Torture Trek

Torture Trek
and Eleven Other Action-Packed Stories of the Wild West
by Ryerson Johnson

Edited by Martin H. Greenberg
and Bill Pronzini

BARRICADE BOOKS INC.
New York

Published by Barricade Books Inc.
150 Fifth Avenue
New York, NY 10011

Library of Congress Cataloging-In-Publication Data

Johnson, Ryerson, 1901-.
    Torture trek and eleven other tales of the Wild West / by Ryerson
Johnson; edited by Martin H. Greenberg and Bill Pronzini.
        p. cm.
    ISBN 1-56980-033-2 (pbk)
    1. West (U.S.)—Social life and customs—Fiction. 2. Frontier and pio-
neer life—West (U.S.)—Fiction. 3. Western stories. I. Greenberg, Martin
Harry. II. Pronzini, Bill. III. Title.
PS3519.028614T67 1995
813'.52—dc20   94-45790
                                                                  CIP

First Printing

Contents

Acknowledgments

This Is the Way It Was

Isn't it a fascinatingly unpredictable world? I had sold three stories to *Adventure* when I met a man who changed the whole course of my writing life.

All I knew about writing when I tackled those first three was to establish a character who wanted something, and run him through a quick succession of interrelated incidents, exciting as I could make them, and dangerous . . . and then pay it all off with an O.Henry surprise ending. I did this against unusual, but familiar backgrounds—coal mines and freight train bumming—crowding in everything bad that could happen to you in a coal mine or on a fast moving manifest freight.

Three stories (the first one, "The Squeeze," in the March 20th, 1926 issue)—and then I met William Byron Mowery who had moved up from the pulps to the slicks, and was selling Canadian Mounted Police serials to *Redbook*.

Mowery told me flatly, "You'll never make a living, writing coal mine and hobo stories. Not a broad enough reader interest in those subjects. You could never sell more than an occasional one. You have to pick a field of popular interest. Westerns . . . or, how about Canadian Mounted Police? I've turned out so many—I could help you with the research. It's a hot field now."

There was something disturbing me. "Westerns and mounties," I said. "You're talking about pulps, aren't you?"

Bill turned aggressively defensive. "What's the matter with pulps?"

"Well, I . . . you know—"

"It's vital, virile fiction. It has all the story fundamentals. And it's a wide-open market. Two hundred magazines out there clamoring for your stuff. There may never be a chance like this again. You can learn your trade in the pulps."

I wasn't convinced. The very word—pulp—rubbed me wrong. I'd always considered pulp magazines to be fodder for borderline illiterates. Their packaging alone had been enough to turn me off—the cheap sulfur-polluted paper and those raw, cornball covers. (I've since come to appreciate inordinately those same fantastic action covers! I have a few artists' oil-painted originals that I accumulated when working for a short time for that grand old man of the pulps, Harry Steeger, at his Popular Publications: copy-editing *Detective Tales, Dime Mystery, The Spider* and *Argosy.* At the peak of his activity Harry had 45 magazines flooding the newsstands—and in a warehouse thousands of cover originals acquired for around $100 apiece. Sadly, that warehouse burned down!)

"How many pulp stories have you read?" Bill inquired.

"Almost none," I said.

"Then how could you know? There are pulps—and there are pulps. I'm talking about *good* pulps. You didn't consider your stories in *Adventure* inferior, did you?"

"No," I said. "They were as good as I could make them—with the limited knowledge I had of fiction put-together—"

"That's what I'm talking about," Bill assured me. "Fiction put-together. Pulp stories are *plot* stories. Six months with your nose to the pulp grindstone, and you can move with confidence into the high-pay slicks."

He was winning me over. He was a pro. I could feel

enthusiasm tingling. "Sounds good," I said, "but about the particular field I'd pick—how about science fiction? I always liked it—"

Bill shook his head no. "It's a low-pay market. And too highly specialized. You don't know your science, do you? And it has a limited readership. *Very* limited. I think the field will grow (Was he ever right!), but its time isn't yet. It's still in its swaddling clothes. Gernsback's *Amazing Stories* is the only magazine of significance, and you'll do well to get more than half a cent a word from him."

He paused, continued almost as if lecturing in one of his classes. (He taught English at the University of Illinois in Urbana.) "At this stage of its development there are just two kinds of science fiction stories, neither of them adequate. You get stories written by academicians and technicians who know their science, but who have no sense of 'story.' And you get professionally written stories by writers who don't know their science. Specializing in that field today, you'd starve."

So I became a writer of Royal Canadian Mounted Police stories.

I didn't know a mounted policeman from a uniformed doorman, but Bill loaned me books and I got more from the library. Official Mounted Police bulletins and a book by Washburton Pike—*The Great Canadian Barren Lands*—supplied the fundamentals. I read for a week and took notes . . . and Bill, out of the kindness of his heart, tutored me in a remarkable story-writing method he had worked out for himself.

In his methodical way, he had broken down many, many magazine short stories, discovered their component parts, noted their common denominators. He analyzed and codified, sorting out 32 elements he felt were common to all effective stories.

With this list of 32, he claimed you could sit coldly

down, tackle the separate points one by one, and when you were finished you'd have a sure-fire story plot. In dramatic detail. Every time! Nothing left to chance or whim. He was so consistent in the pre-composition effort that he even codified the emotional content the finished story would have.

Lured on by his promise of quick and positive success, I knuckled down to it, putting together practice plots. They creaked and cranked. Clumsy machinery. Lifeless as a wooden cigar store Indian.

The effort of putting together these specialized outlines violated all my instincts. I much preferred to dive into a story, gut-level, and see what happened.

Bill scowled at that. "Unprofessional! A wasteful way of writing. Hit and miss. For every one that jells by that method, a dozen fail. Leave that for the poets and literati."

"But the inspirational story that did well would be something special, wouldn't it?"

He nodded. "Sure. But what kind of a living can you make selling a story once in a while? You want to write for a living, don't you? Writing as a way of life?"

Now *I* nodded—very affirmatively.

"You've probably heard it said," he went on, "that true art ignores the audience. Maybe. But not if you're writing to make a living."

For Bill Mowery the public was a stern, unforgiving, and perpetually overshadowing presence. "Forget about pleasing yourself," Bill said, "and write for the market. Never let the reader slip out of your awareness. Strictly objective writing. You—the writer—don't exist. Not to the reader, and not even to yourself. You don't intrude; you don't insert yourself in any manner anywhere in your story."

He seemed to be looking a little past me. "Actually, there *are* two ways you can go. Precious pieces for the 'little mags'—the university literary magazines such as *Prairie Schooner* and *Yale Review*. They won't pay you anything, but after you place enough with them you'll get letters from publishers wanting to see your next novel. In the meantime you have to live, and you won't be able to do it by writing.

"The other way is my way. The scientific method applied to your typing fingers. You approach the subject of writing analytically. You do a story so carefully contrived that you contrivedly hide the contriving. And you sell what you want to do—writing. And you've got the rest of your life to go artistic if you want to."

I caught his point. I kept turning out those 32-point outlines—pre-comps, he called them. One day Bill said I had one good enough to use as a blueprint for a finished story.

"Write it," he said, then added sternly, "Don't deviate. You've got everything in that pre-comp you need to write a salable story. Don't go off chasing rabbits. Stay with the story plan you know is sound."

I wrote it—though I had it practically written before I started. I had twice the wordage in that pre-comp that I could use in the finished story. It was largely a matter of squeezing it down and imparting the flow.

"Cougar Kelly Gets a Break." Cougar Kelly was a rookie Royal Canadian Mounted Policeman. *Adventure* turned the story down, I think because of too much unskilled emphasis on technique, and not enough reality-feel. But Clayton Publishers, a competitor of *Adventure* in the general action field, bought it the next time out for their *Wide World Adventures*. They paid *Adventure*'s rate of two cents a word.

Two cents a word for 5000 words—$100. To put that price in a time frame: it figured out to two or three times the weekly wage of the magazine editors who read the story and shaped it up for publication.

Clayton was blue-ribbon among pulp publishers. They started you at two cents, and after your first few stories, raised you a tenth of a cent a word to a top of three cents. No other house did this across the board.

In fairly quick succession then I wrote "Caribou Gold," "All Trees and Snow" . . . "The Carcajou and the Loup Garou" . . . "The Eskimo Express" . . . "The Dangerous Dan McGrew," and others—all Canadian Mounted, or northern trapping or mining stories. They sold the first or second time out to Fiction House's *Northwest Stories*, Doubleday's *West*, Street & Smith's *Top Notch*, and Clayton's *Ace High*.

It wasn't long before the bottom went out of the Mounted Police business. I don't know why, but people lost interest in the Far North.

I had to find another field. The largest group of magazines on the newsstands were westerns. There must have been well over 50 titles. I "went west" on a trip that lasted nearly 20 years.

The switch from northerns to westerns wasn't much of a problem. The West of the magazines was a very limited world. You could choose to write gun-town stories, gun-trail stories, ranch stories, an occasional gold mining or railroad/stagecoach story . . . and that was about it. I thought all I'd have to do was read a batch of western pulps . . . and I was right.

I started in, reading first to get the story, reading a second time to get the feel of the presentation, the formula, the pacing, and to soak up some of the jargon and fictional conventions. For instance: they rarely called a revolver a revolver. It was a six-gun, six-shooter, 45 Colt's, shooting iron, smoke pole . . . You could invent a likely name of your own if you wanted to.

A cowboy was a cowboy sometimes, but he was also a ranny, puncher, waddy, cowpoke, ranch-hand . . . A ranch was almost always a "spread." The Box-K spread, the Bar X . . .

Such colorful little aberrations of the language took a while to absorb. But it's something you have to confront on working with any new background.

I started getting on with my first western story after about a week of intensive reading of western pulps, and taking notes. I didn't sell my first one, but I sold all the rest, right up to the last one. The last one—uncounted hundreds of western stories later—was bucking an almost vanished market.

After I got well into the western field I did do some background reading, and settled upon two books. I found that I could get nearly all the information I needed to write acceptable western stories from Rollins' *The Cowboy*, and Webb's *The Great Plains*. Webb supplied the historical perspective—the progression from open-range ranching to the barb-wire fencing era. (The "civilizing" effects of barbaric barbed wire! I wrote a novel about it: *Barb-Wire*.) Rollins, on the other hand, was meticulous in revealing the day-by-day details of cowboy life, everything from what he ate for breakfast to what he rode and wore—and his preferred branding and shooting irons.

My first western sale was to trusty old *Ace High*—a gun-trail story: "The Yucca Kid"—although Street & Smith's *Western Story* ultimately became my most dependable market, along with *Short Stories* and *Star Western*.

I stayed pretty much with westerns until TV kicked the pulps off the stands. Within three or four years after TV established itself comfortably in American homes, western magazines bit the dust. It was easier to drink your beer and watch *Bonanza* or *Have Gun, Will Travel.* You didn't even have to turn pages.

I should mention an alternative way of writing stories. Good old Bill Mowery was also coaching two of my friends, Lloyd Eric Reeve and George Shaftel, introducing them into the pulp world. The three of us would gather at Lloyd's apartment sometimes. Lloyd's wife, Alice, poured tea and listened quietly while we pitched the virtues of the Mowery Method.

It became increasingly apparent that she was antagonistic to it. "It kills your creativity," she insisted. "Bill's making automatons of you all!"

This was sacrilege. We argued with her—three against one.

We couldn't budge her. "Bill's way allows no expression of verve, spontaneity, freshness . . . No human warmth—"

"Yes, it does! All of that's structured into the outline—"

"You can structure emotion?"

"Sure . . . sure . . . sure. Look at the record. We're selling."

But then Lloyd's record became not so good. He ran into a spell where nothing was selling. He dropped in at my place one day, gloomy and discouraged. "I've got the promise of a job driving a truck," he said. "I start tomorrow."

But Lloyd's truck driving career never wheeled out. In that afternoon's mail he received two story checks.

And Alice?

Soon afterwards she sat down at the typewriter, and

just out of her head and feelings—no outlining, no conscious striving—wrote a pleasant little story about some people with problems, and sold it to *Good Housekeeping* for $900. And she kept on doing this!

So . . . each to his own. You pays your money and you makes your choice. The rest of us stuck to the proven Mowery Method. The planned approach. Cerebral.

I realized later that what we had done was swap creativity for skill satisfaction. And as time went on I realized that to some extent I was working against myself. Bill, an iconoclastic loner, a complex man with deeply buried fears, needed order, structure, and boundaries within which he could safely and securely operate. Temperamentally, I think I was his exact opposite. Rules and boundaries stifled me. I like "change," and a little insecurity puts zest into living. So increasingly I have loosened up in my writing.

But I will always be grateful to Bill for getting me securely enmeshed in the fiction writing business. Action fiction in the beginning. Pulp fiction—a never-never land that existed only in the glowing imagination of the writer, and the transient "suspension of disbelief" of the reader. Bigger than life. Adult fairy stories.

These days when I start a story I still know where it's going to end, and I know my main characters and what they want and who's trying to keep them from getting it. I know most of the high points along the way. Beyond that, I'm inclined to "let it roll." In the writing, if the story takes a hop in an unplanned direction, sometimes I go along with it.

In any case, with all its insecurity, the time-and-place freedom of the freelance life has made it all wonderfully worthwhile. It's been a high, good life. It still is! When

the pulps phased out I stayed barnstorm freelancing—
trade and textbook, child and adult, long and short—
everything from comics to Encyclopedia Britannica.

But bright in remembrance is that incredible era when
all those pulp magazines were flapping hungry covers for
copy. For better or worse, I know they have influenced my
writing to this day.

THE AMERICAN FICTION GUILD

The second time I went from Illinois to New York "because
that's where the writers and markets are," I travelled in
style, "riding the cushions" *inside* the train. It could have
well been the same Empire State Express on the New York
Central Railroad where, the first time, I'd tied myself on
top, "riding the deck," and gulping smoke and cinders.

Upward mobility, I think they're calling it today.

That first time in New York I didn't make it as a writer.
Just to keep eating I had to spend most of the time shoveling snow for the city, driving a milk wagon for Borden,
and managing a loading wharf operation for U.S. Gyp-
sum.

But the second time, with a dozen or more pulp sales
under my belt, the white flame of expectation was shared
with a feeling of quiet confidence that I had the writer's
trade firmly in hand. I arrived in the fall of '33 with very
little money in pocket, but I didn't look for a job. I got
a room at $4.50 a week (about the price you would pay
in New York to park for an hour) in a rundown Times
Square rooming house on 44th Street. There were still a
few of them left—old brownstones that hadn't been broken
up and hauled away to make room for shining new hotels.

I put shirts and socks and underwear in a rickety

drawer, draped my valued collection of carefully chosen
neckties over a coat hanger (those were the days when we
wore neckties, and I like 'em loud), hung up my go-to-
magazine-offices suit that in my younger days would have
been the go-to-church suit, decked the portable and
started writing.

These were still Depression days and it was tough selling
anything anywhere. My main market, Clayton Co.'s *Ace
High*, had gone out of business and I had to crack some
new markets. It was disappointingly slow-going. I had to
resort sometimes to Bernarr MacFadden's Penny Restaurants. MacFadden published *Physical Culture Magazine*
and *Liberty*. He once paid President Calvin Coolidge a
dollar a word, a fantastically impressive price at that
time. On this occasion Coolidge wasn't sparing words;
according to the scuttlebutt on Publisher's Row, his article
ran twice as long as *Liberty* wanted it.

MacFadden was health oriented. At his Penny Restaurants the only available "coffee" was made of toasted
grains and chicory. But it only cost two cents. For a few
cents more, the main meal staples were steamed whole
grains, dried fruit, and various kinds of such. You ate it
standing up, with your plate on a narrow shelf. The food
kept you circulating; MacFadden performed a valuable
service. The next step down were the missions' free soup
kitchens. With MacFadden you paid for it and "kept your
self respect."

For a couple of weeks on one occasion I narrowly
averted the soup kitchens, although I had checks for two
Street & Smith western stories in the mail. The postman
left the mail at the bottom of the steps at this fleabag of
a rooming house. Somebody evidently picked up the envelope, but chickened out on trying to cash them. Street
& Smith issued new checks.

Street & Smith's *Western Story* settled down to being my best market, with the company's *Top Notch*, *Cowboy Stories* and *Wild West Weekly* providing dependable sell-off markets. If you can't get two cents, take one. Some of the boys went all the way down-river to the half-cent and even the rare quarter-cent markets. I never went below a cent. I'd keep sending it around. Rewrite if I had to. Sooner or later it slotted in somewhere. With upwards of a hundred magazines flapping hungry covers for copy, if you wrote a careful story, you couldn't miss.

As far as I know, nothing like that dependable market exists today, except perhaps in the comics field. I sold, literally, every pulp story I ever wrote except the first one and the last one. That first one wasn't quite right. The last one was bucking a vanishing market. I still have that one somewhere—one of the Len Siringo town-tamer series that ran in Harry Steeger's *Star Western*. (Don't ask me about the score on slick stories; sales there have run consistently about one in five.)

There were many more cent-a-word markets than there were cent-and-a-half and two-cent markets. *Adventure*, *Blue Book*, *Western Story Weekly*, *Popular* and *Black Mask*—and the Clayton group, while it lasted—were about the only ones paying two cents. And sometimes *Argosy* and *Short Story*.

A fast writer could do all right with the cent-a-word market. You could do a fifteen or twenty thousand word novelette for the cent-market in the time it took to turn out a 5000-word short story for the two-cent market. I never was a fast writer and I figured it paid me to do the careful two-cent story.

Writing is a lonesome business. You sit in your room with your typewriter and the four walls, and whether you're revealing and interpreting, as in factual writing—or dreaming up new worlds, as in fiction writing—you're still living your life second-hand. I needed to get out and meet some people; particularly, I needed to meet some other writers. There were supposed to be several hundred in and around New York. I didn't know *any*.

I had heard about an organization called "The American Fiction Guild," a pulp-writer's professional organization that scheduled weekly luncheon meetings at Rosoff's restaurant just off Times Square on, I think, 43rd Street. A writer was supposed to have sold 100,000 words of fiction to be eligible to join. I hadn't, but I was climbing close.

I showed up one noon in my go-to-magazine-offices suit and my most impressive necktie, and with a check in my pocket for a story to *Argosy* in case anybody should wonder. Arthur Burks, president of the organization and one of its founders, greeted me pleasantly and introduced me around.

Sixty pulp writers all in one place! That initial experience was a little overwhelming. I didn't get acquainted with all 60 at that first luncheon, but I made a good start.

Impressive to me were the dyed-in-the-woodpulp professionals, the "typewriter burners." There was Lester Dent who did the monthly magazine novel, *Doc Savage*. Walter Gibson—twice monthly *The Shadow*. Arthur Leo Zagat—the "horror-story man." George Bruce—air/war. Joe Archibald—sports and war, as I remember. Doris Knight and Harriet Bradfield who worked both sides of the editorial desk on lovepulp. Baynard Kendrick who had a blind detective series running in *Black Mask*. Ron Hubbard—the future Scientology/Dianetics guru. Paul Ernst—the future *Avenger*. (Ernst, incidentally, wrote a short story for *Argosy* that I still remember: "To Heaven Standing Up." It could have appeared in any good slick magazine.)

Include Damon Knight and Theodore Sturgeon who quickly soared to science fiction fame. (Who remembers now that Damon eased into his writing career with a copy editing job on *Dime Western* and *Star Western*? We moved around; pulp editing and pulp writing were sometimes interchangeable. I knew I would eventually have to make a switch from westerns, and I chose the detective/mystery field. Around 1940 I went to work for Popular Publications on *Detective Tales* and *Dime Mystery*. My desk was next to Damon's, and on the other side was Harry Widmer who had the *Aces* line. I took over the job from Robert Turner who had decided to go back to freelancing. A few months later when I figured I'd absorbed the detective/ mystery pattern, I quit to start writing them and Bob returned to his old job. But he didn't stay long either. He went to Hollywood to do "Shotgun Slade" and a bunch of good paperback novels. He also did that book on the pulp magazine scene with the marvelous title: *Some Of My Best Friends are Writers, But I Wouldn't Want My Daughter to Marry One.*)

Let's see . . . who else? Ted Tinsley was there. Ted was in with Art Burks in founding the organization. Chuck Verral, who hadn't yet started to write his *Bill Barnes* books. Robert Arthur—mystery pulp, radio, Hitchcock Hollywood, everything. William Bogart, who went on to ghost some *Doc Savage* novels for Lester Dent. Jack D'Arcy (D. L. Champion) who wrote *The Phantom Detective* for Leo Margulies at Standard Publications.

A little sidelight on Jack. He was living the good life for a while at Tortola in the Virgin Islands when he was contacted by the producer of the "Amos and Andy" radio show, who had read a story of Jack's in *Black Mask*. He liked Jack's sense of humor, he said, and invited him to come to Hollywood at his expense and write gags for the show.

Jack went out. He suffered periodically from arthritis, and he limped into the studio.

"What's the matter with your leg?" someone asked him.

"Arthritis."

The man got on the phone to a friend. "Hi Frank . . . who's the best arthritis doc in Beverly Hills?"

The friend gave him a name and the man phoned again, setting up an appointment. Right now! They get things done in Hollywood. Right now.

Jack was limousined to his appointment . . . and in an hour or so reappeared at the studio. The man at the desk stared at him, disbelieving.

"You're still limping!"

The man's reaction confirmed everything Jack had ever thought about the money-buys-miracles mentality of Hollywood, and he went into his introductory session with something less than enthusiasm.

The way we got it later from Jack: "The gag writers sat around a long table. They've got me in there with them. 'Amos' sat at one end of the table, and 'Andy' at the other. Someone would throw out a feeler on a wisecrack. Someone else would pick it up. The idea would bounce back and forth, being modified and refined. When it was all wrapped up . . . when the boys could go no farther with it . . . Amos and Andy bought in. If they liked it they held a thumb up. If they didn't like it they punched a thumb down. If both of them had a thumb up, the gag was in."

That one session was enough for Jack. He came limping back to New York . . . and on to Tortola.

A couple more at the meeting: Frank Gruber of "Johnny Fletcher" fame and Day Keene. Gruber went on to Hollywood, where he wrote for the "Wells Fargo" and "Shotgun Slade" TV shows.

And Day Keene. A good story about Day. When I was editing at Popular, they bought everything of Day Keene's that came in, even if they didn't have an immediate spot for it. He was so good, they didn't want any competing magazine to get him!

All right, and so how's this for an example of the uncertainties a freelance writer faces in editorial decisions? Popular Publications bought the title from Munsey to that grand old queen of the pulps, *Argosy*. Popular had plans to turn the magazine into a semi-slick. Day Keene at the time was running a very successful series character in Popular's *Detective Tales*. The novelettes chronicled the street adventures of Silent Smith—"the silver-haired gambler of Broadway." Executive editor Rogers Terrill urged Day to write a long Silent Smith novelette for the new, upgraded *Argosy*.

Impressed that *Argosy* was scheduled to be a notch above the pulps, Day extended himself and brought in a piece he considered to be a quality story.

Rog regretfully turned it down. "Sorry, Day. It just isn't *Argosy* caliber. Too pulpy. But I can use it for *Detective Tales*."

Since Day had spent a few more hours than usual in working up this story, he turned down the offer and gave the story to his agent, Sid Sanders.

Sid sold it the first time out to *Good Housekeeping* for, if I remember right, $4600. Big, big money in those days.

There's a sequel to this story. Day blinked, wondering how long this kind of story money had been floating around. He sat down and read a few copies of *Good House-*

keeping to feel out their style, then, at their urging, wrote another Silent Smith story beamed right at their market.

Good Housekeeping turned it down.

Rogers Terrill ultimately bought it. But not for *Detective Tales*. Day Keene was a slick-paper name now. Rog bought the story for the new upgraded *Argosy.*

To get back to the fiction guild: Also at this luncheon were all those other fired-up, hungry ones, coming on fast. Charley Green (C. V. Tawney), Steve Fisher, Mort Weisinger who piloted *Superman* and *Batman* comics for so many years, Otto Binder, the *Captain Marvel* man and *Space Magazine* publisher, Bruno Fischer . . . so many.

The organization also included a sprinkling of editors and agents. Bee Jones and Eve Woodburn. Pauline Bloom. Leo Margulies, who headed up the large Standard group of magazines; and Orlin Tremaine from Street & Smith's *Top Notch*. Lurton "Count" Blassingame—called Count because he looked like one. Count soon afterwards moved into smooth paper magazine and book agenting. Otis Adelbert Kline, and that indefatigable pulp agent, Ed Bodin.

New York City held definite advantages for a freelancer. The American Fiction Guild was one of them. It was the most effective writer's organization I ever belonged to. Through it you made direct contacts with writers, agents and editors. And in addition to those weekly luncheon get-togethers, the AFG sponsored a monthly magazine that was mailed out to members everywhere. It carried profiles of the members and current news of the trade. The Guild also mailed out weekly postcards containing hot market tips.

Webs for One . . .

GOLD BOWED THE little man's back—60 pounds of gold.

The weight forced his bear-paw racquets deep into powdery snow and made the going excruciatingly hard. Let the pack straps gall! It was a good hurt. At first Alf Newberry had only wished it would hurt more. More hurt would mean more weight of gold. And the more gold a man had, the bigger twist he could take on the world's tail when he got outside.

Of course, he wasn't going to get outside. The Canadian barren grounds, this great lone land that sprawled in frozen silence across the top of a continent, would never let him go. He could read his death warrant clearly in his empty food pack, the 40-below cold, and the two days' travel yet required to put him on Bent Willow Creek at timberline.

Not any one thing, but a lot of little things had tipped the balance the wrong way. That roving Yellowknife Indian with whom he had shared his scant food supply . . . But what else could a fellow do? The Indian was starving. No way to have predicted he would repay by stealing most of the rifle cartridges.

Right to the end, the little things had kept bunching up to spell northern death. His last bullet, fired at a snowshoe rabbit . . . and that streak of white lightning in the shape of an Arctic fox detaching itself from the snow hummock. The fox had been stalking too. And it was the fox that got the rabbit.

Alf had thrown away the rifle to lighten his load. Now it was time to throw away his gold.

He made the decision calmly, after falling twice within the same five minutes. On this rolling rock-ribbed tundra, every snow-pillowed half acre looked like every other half acre. It had been a six-year job to trace the gold through the cracks and crannies of frost-split granite to its ultimate hiding place.

Six years—and he could lose it all in six minutes! But life alone was the stake now.

After his last fall, he stayed down while he groped stiff-handed in the snow to loosen his pack straps. He didn't make much headway, and a small panic touched him. A man with his strength too far run out could die in the North, anchored to his gold!

But Alf Newberry, being a little man, had long since learned the rashness of butting into things full tilt, whether it was a bigger man who opposed him, or simply the waiting hostile North. There were things fully as potent as force. There was timing and there was head work. He quit his exhausting struggle with the incubus that rode his back; and he wriggled his wool-gloved hand from its huge covering mitt of moosehide, and from an inner recess of his parka, brought out a pint whiskey bottle. Only about enough whiskey left for one good jolt. But it was north-country liquor, supercharged stuff with an alcoholic content so high that the coldest weather couldn't freeze it.

Alf knew how to take it. In nips. That way it would feed through his jaded body with a reviving fire. He'd get out from under this gold all right, and he'd go a long way yet on his feet. When he flopped on his face for the last time—well, that would be something else again. He'd save the last swallow for then. Cold, whiskey, and fatigue would anesthetize him. He'd die just like going to sleep.

Not that that made it easier to get used to the idea. Why, he'd hardly begun to live! Tramping the world's shrinking gold frontiers ever since he'd been old enough to carry a pack and an ore hammer, he'd been lonely, with the good things always beckoning from over the hump of the next hill. So lonely that sometimes over his fire, in the drag of the night wind, he'd hear laughter. Soft laughter from the woman never loved because never known; shrill gay laughter from children, shadow-born; gusty laughter from mellowed friends that in his will-o'-the-wisp wandering over the back trails he'd never stopped long enough to meet.

And now, just when it had given golden promise of arriving somewhere, his trail had run out—

Or had it?

His eyes, gray-dull and expressionless, took quick fire. His head on its scrawny neck poked ludicrously from his parka hood, and his nostrils flared. Thin and acrid in the cold air, a trace of coal smoke had wafted to him. Coal smoke? Why not! There was coal in this country as well as gold. The trick was to find it . . .

The low shale cliff was plastered 10 feet deep with snow. But Alf Newberry found it. Trembling in near exhaustion, he had only to push aside the wolfhide coverings in order to enter the cave and embrace life instead of death. But he held back. The assurance of life had made the gold of prime importance again. A little man, Alf Newberry had early bought into a game where bone and muscle held blue chip values. The pushing around he'd had to take from bigger men had made him wary. Six years scrounging the top bleak quarter of the globe for gold . . . He didn't propose to lose it now in a single unguarded moment.

With concentrated effort, he wrung his shoulders free from the rucksack loops, let the burden of gold plump deep in a drift. Only then did he move to poke his head beyond those wolfhide coverings.

He stood silently at first, peering inside the cave. Rime was white and heavy on his parka hood where it fringed his gnome-like face. He appeared, perhaps, not quite real.

At least the man who sat on the shale ledge, staring back at him through the haze of coal smoke, seemed to have doubts. The man was a giant. Compared to Alf he was. His pale eyes stared with a curious burning from under a tangle of bushy brows, shaggy hair. A six-months' beard inundated the rest of his face. Alf surmised that under its dirt and soot the shrubbery might be blond.

The giant stirred.

"Where the hell'd you come from?"

His voice from the back of the cave was a hollow booming. It sounded as though he were trying hard to believe what he saw.

Alf lifted his hand in a weak sweep toward the North. Words pushed through his frost-scabbed lips: "Headin' for timberline. Got a grub cache on Bent Willow Creek." He shook his head. "I'd never made it. Don't mind tellin' you, brother—runnin' onto you has saved my life."

The big man kept staring while Alf moved deeper inside the cave, shaking off his mitts, and blinking his eyes to accustom himself to the smoky gloom. A tiny coal fire flickered on the floor. He hunkered close to it.

"Make yourself at home," the brooding giant said, and laughed. It wasn't an insane laugh. But there was a flat mirthlessness about it that put Alf on his guard.

"What are you, man or boy?" the big one spoke again. "Pound for pound, inch for inch, I'd make two of you."

"You wouldn't miss it much," Alf conceded.

"You're all beat in, ain't you?"

"It's been tough goin'," Alf further conceded.

"Ain't you got a gun?"

"Threw it away to lighten my pack."

"What pack?"

"Unloaded that too."

There was a taut eagerness in the big fellow's voice when he put the next question.

"Snowshoes?"

"I kicked the webs off outside here."

Something like a satisfied animal grunt sounded faintly from the big man's throat.

Alf said wearily, "Let me ask you one, brother. How long's it till dinner time?"

"Hungry?"

"Starved."

"Makes it tough," the big man said. "I only got enough for myself."

He hadn't changed his tone. But the words were as damning to Alf Newberry's hopes of living as though a black-garbed judge had resounded sentence: ". . . hanged by the neck until dead."

Alf blew on his fingers. "Like that, huh?"

"Like that," the big man said. Surprisingly, then, he made a wheedling attempt at self justification. "I been sittin' here myself waitin' to die. Run across this coal ledge last summer, so I based out of here. When the snow clamped down, I holed in. Coal outcrops right in my parlor, like you can see. Lucky thing for me. I lost my gun and my snowshoes right after freeze-up when I went through the ice."

Alf could understand the other's special interest now in the matter of snowshoes. And the laugh—sardonic, as well it might be, because in both their cases the North had rendered its judgment, and it was the same judgment: Death for Alf Newberry because he had no food. Death for the big fellow here because he had no snowshoes.

There was, of course, a corollary to that. Each man was only half a man; together they were whole.

The big man heaved to his feet. Even with his shoulders humped, his bushy head scraped the roof. "Think I'll have a look at them snowshoes of yours," he said.

"Wait a minute," Alf said. All his life pushed around by bigger men—but one certain result of it had been to sharpen his wits. He made a stab at breaking up decision before it might crystallize. He said earnestly, "You're not seein' it all the way through, brother. We can both live."

"Yeah?"

"Easy," Alf pressed. "Divvy a little of your grub with me, just enough for a two-day trip to the creek where my food cache is. I'll lug enough stuff back for you to last out the winter here if you want."

"Yeah?" The dangling arms swung slowly. "How do I know you'd come back?"

"You'd have to take my word for it, brother."

"I don't take nobody's word for nothin'."

It had been a pass at something; that was all. The big grizzly, the way Alf sized him up, ran his life by hard and fast rules, with greed—and consequently suspicion—high among the motive powers. Solid beef had always been enough to get him by, so he'd never felt prodded to develop much imagination. Hard to reach a man like that.

"We'll gamble," Alf said desperately. "How about it? Your grub sack against my snowshoes."

Agreement came readily. Too readily, was Alf's uneasy thought. It was as though the big man knew he had nothing to lose.

"We can toss a coin," the big man said. "I got one. United States dollar I always kept for luck."

He went ahead and made the toss, caught the twirling dollar in the chunky palm of one hand, and spanked his other hand down flat across it.

"Call it."

"Heads."

The big man opened his dirt-slick hands. The dollar was showing heads all right.

"I win," Alf said, but without elation. That was because he was more than half primed for what happened next.

The big man pulled a long skinning knife from his belt. The firelight glinted on the blade in the same dim way it had on the dollar. Cold decision flared in the pale eyes, and the big man moved in on Alf.

Alf fumbled his own knife out and brandished it. But he was backing away. What else could he do? His nerves screamed the question. Weak as a rabbit, and showing only half the other's size—

The big man kept moving in, crouched low, stumping his feet down wide apart for balance, his tree trunk body weaving as he took his inches-short steps. The knife in his blocky fist kept fanning slowly in front of him as he came. Alf, feinting desperately, gave ground as he had to. When he felt his shoulder brushing the wolfhide flaps at the cave opening, he went all-out on another gamble.

This big grizzly, he reasoned, wasn't a natural killer. He would kill now, but only because of his stubborn belief that his life depended on it. That was why, undoubtedly, he had agreed to gamble in the first place. A win would have quieted his conscience, settled everything for him without the need for violence.

Alf reached back through the door flaps and threw his knife as far as he could into the snow. He showed his hands, flat out, and empty.

"I quit!" he shouted.

The big man quit too. He straightened up. He seemed vaguely pleased. "Glad you got some sense," he scolded. "I didn't want to kill you."

"What do you think you're doin' by leavin' me here to starve?"

"That's only your hard luck."

Alf stared bitterly. "The twists a man can put on his reasonin'!"

The big man clumped about, pulled a small canvas bag from a wall cranny, and sat down with it on the ledge. He untied the knot at the loose end of the bag and took out a piece of caribou jerky. With his knife he hacked off a little of the hard dry meat. He crammed it in his mouth and chewed with relish.

Alf's own gnawing hunger put a weakening tremor over him, and he could feel the saliva jet from under his tongue.

"Never like to start a long trip on an empty stomick," the big man offered, talking thickly through the raw meat that swelled, with mastication, to fill his mouth. "Figure I got a week's hard trek to the closest caribou hunters' camp below timberline."

When he finished, he put the remainder of the jerky away and retied the knot in the bag's loose end.

"Better tie it tighter," Alf told him. "I might make a grab and open it."

The big man didn't read any sarcasm in Alf's scraping

voice. He reacted literally; gave the knot another yank.
Then he put the food bag down beside his gold pan that
was full of melted snow water, and keeping one eye on Alf,
he lowered his face to drink. After that he stood up, carefully wiped off his beard, moved about and pulled on a
mackinaw, and over that a fur parka.

Alf rummaged inside his own parka and brought out
his bottle. He held it out.

"What's that?"

"Whiskey."

"What you handin' it to me for?"

"You're the one who's got somethin' to celebrate."

The big man came over and took the bottle. He shook
it skeptically, held it to the light and watched the bubbles
chase to the top and disappear. He opened the bottle,
smelled it, tilted it cautiously to his lips.

He whipped it down. "It's got the old sting," he said.
"It's whiskey, all right." Then his voice turned whiney-
mean with suspicion. "I get it—you think you're goin' to
soften me up. Makin' me presents. Yeah. Well, that's out,
see? I'm strong, and not only in my muscles. My will
power. If I have to let somebody die to save my own life—
well, that's how it is, see?"

He lifted the bottle, disposed of half the liquor with
one big noisy swallow.

Alf said doubtfully, "You think you ought to drink the
rest? You're goin' out in the cold, and you know what that
can do to a drunk man."

"To a runt like you maybe," the big man said. "Not to
me. When that much whiskey makes me drunk, I'll sign
the pledge." He drained the rest of the whiskey and let
his breath out in a noisy *wo-oo-oo-sh.*

Alf sighed, and went over and dropped down on the
ledge on the side of the water pan that was away from the

food bag. He lowered his face and drank deliberately, tipping the shallow pan a little, the better to get at the water.

"Sure," the big man said, "I'll drink the whiskey; you take the chaser. Just don't get inside of monkey range with my food bag, that's all." He laughed in that flat short way. "Them scrawny fingers of yours. They couldn't untie the bag anyhow. When I tie somethin', it stays tied."

He made a roll of his eiderdown sleeping bag, then picked up a small rucksack from the corner. He hefted it as though he liked to feel its solid weight, and the greed was naked in his pale eyes. "I got 30 pounds here. Figures around 16 thousand. I did all right, huh?"

Alf lifted his mouth from the pan. Water dripped from the point of his thin nose and from his lightly stubbled chin. "Fair," he said. "But I beat the North for twice that much."

"Yeah—to hear you tell it."

"I'll show you."

Alf got up and ducked outside. The big man came and watched narrowly from the cave opening. Alf dug his rucksack from the drift and dragged it back through the snow to the cave. He opened it up on the floor, revealing the tightly packed skin pokes. He loosened the *babiche* strings on one of them. Raw, new gold in dust and nuggets of cornmeal yellow glowed softly in the firelight.

"Thirty thousand, easy," Alf said.

The big man was breathing hard, his pale eyes squeezed half shut and staring. Alf dipped up a handful of the gold, let it stream back through his fingers. Six years to accumulate it, grain by grain, speck by speck. Now he dusted his hands prodigally against his sides.

"Don't do that!" the big man jabbed.

"Why not? Mine, ain't it, to waste if I want?" Alf looked

up with sly malice. "You know what I got a notion to do? Take this whole 60 pounds of gold and scatter it on the snow. I'd have me one high minute that way."

The big man pushed threateningly close, and Alf stood up and moved back. His frost-cracked lips were bent in a crooked grin, and a slow fire pierced the dull gray of his eyes. "Don't worry," he said. "I give you the gold. I give it to you before you have to bash my skull in and take it away from me. I'll make it easy for your conscience, brother."

The big man looked relieved in about the same degree as when Alf had thrown away the knife. "Go bring those snowshoes in," he ordered.

Alf brought them in and the big man tried them on in the middle of the floor. Right after that he set about loading the gold on his back. The straps on Alf's pack were too tight. They bunched the parka fur at the neck, bound the shoulders.

"Here, I'll fix it for you," Alf said.

Like a mule being diamond hitched to a pack load, the big man stood, bowed over patiently, while Alf worked to center the load and adjust the straps. But as a precaution the big man had sheathed his knife on the outside of his parka, and as a further precaution he kept the knife in his hand while Alf worked over him.

His voice carried that self-justifying whine again when he said, "You're still figurin' you can get around me. But I told you when you gave me the whiskey, and I'm tellin' you now: I'm strong, see? Sixty pounds of gold, and it ain't buyin' you one mouthful to eat."

Alf stood back, said reflectively, "I donno; you think you ought to carry both these gold packs? You think you're strong enough? They'll add up 90 pounds. You're too heavy for these webs of mine anyhow, and the weight

of the gold will push 'em even deeper in the snow. Liftin'
'em up and sockin' 'em down—they'll feel like boulders
tied to your feet—"

"What the hell are you, my mother?" the big man
flared. "I'm the one that's goin' to leave here and live.
You're goin' to stay and die. Ain't that enough for you to
worry about?"

"I died out there on the trail," Alf said. His voice was
worn, his pinched face expressionless.

"Huh? You nuts or what?"

"I mean I had my mind all set for it. The worst was
then. This is only a kind of tailin' off. I don't feel much
now."

The big man said, "Huh!" and moved across the cave
to the ledge where his food bag lay. The fire had gone
down. In the smoky gloom he didn't see the puddle of
water on the ledge until he put his hand in it. Then he
swore.

"You splashed water all over the ledge," he said, accus-
ingly.

"It was kind of dark," Alf said. "I couldn't see good.
Must of tilted the pan too far when I was drinkin'."

The big man sheathed his knife and held the food bag
away from him and wrung a drop or two of water from
it.

Alf moved closer, peering. "It ain't wet but only on the
loose end, is it? Water won't hurt the jerky none."

It was outside in the snow, with the big man loaded and
standing on Alf's snowshoes and ready to go, that Alf
resorted to downright appeal. His thin face puckered suddenly, and his words poured out in bursts:

"Before it's too late, think what you're doin', man! It
doesn't have to be this way. Nobody has to die. We can
both live. Just let me take the webs, like I said before,

and enough grub to get me to my cache. I'll come back to you. We can both live—

The big man broke savagely into his pleading. "I thought that iron nerve of yours was too good to last. Couldn't take it, huh? You had to get down and beg!"

Inside the parka Alf's thin shoulders were hunched against the gray cold. "Believe me," he chattered, "if I'm beggin', it's for you."

The big man snorted in derision. "You don't scare worth a damn, runt." But then he hedged the bet enough to ask sharply, "What you talkin' at anyhow?"

Alf's arms were swinging wide in an Eskimo slap against his sides. It was a good way to keep the circulation up. "Not any one thing," he said gently. "It's hardly ever any one thing, is it? Just a lot of little things workin' together."

"You're goin' nuts," the big man growled. "So long— and thanks for the gold." He lifted a snowshoe and leaned into the step.

That was when Alf made his play. "Just remember I gave you your chance." He mouthed the words as he lurched forward, with one of his swinging hands raking across the fur of the big man's parka to the place where his knife was sheathed.

Alf got the knife. The trouble was, he couldn't stay on his feet. The big man's elbow swerved around, striking and knocking him down. He kept himself tumbling and rolling through the snow until he was momentarily out of the other's reach. And he held on to the knife.

The big man waddled around on the webs and stood there, humped under the gold, watching warily while Alf floundered upright in the snow. Buried in whiskered stubble, the big man's lips pushed out words:

"Not any one thing, but a lot of little ones, huh? I'm gettin' it now. You gave me your whiskey. Yeah. And loaded me down with your gold and put me on your runt webs. Yeah. Then you stand there beggin', and with your teeth chatterin', and lookin' helpless, and throw me off my guard. Then you take my knife. . . . All right, you got my knife. Let's see you try to kill me with it."

He stood waiting on his tree-stump legs, his long arms dangling in their bulk of fur. His breath in the 40-below cold dropped past his knees in steamy feathers.

"Come on," he urged again. "You're goin' to find out I'm not drunk, and that I got what it takes to move around under 90 pounds of gold. It ain't goin' to anchor me down, like you thought. It'll only be like some armor plate instead. It'll help me. These runt webs of yours are sinkin' some under me, yeah, but not as far as them pipe-stem legs of yours are bogged down. Wallowin' in the snow, you'll never get that knife in me through all the clothes I got on, before I can knock it out of your hands and break your neck. But if you want to try it, come on."

Alf stood crouched in snow halfway to his hips, and as the heartbreak truth of what the big man said got through to him, his hand which held the knife began to sag.

The big man saw, and snapped, "Drop the knife, or I'll move in on you. You won't get far without snowshoes. I'll kill you with my two hands."

A moment more Alf hesitated, his face in a tortured knot. Then his arm swung back and he threw the knife as far away as he could. It drove into a drift and disappeared.

"Go dive in that drift and bring me back my knife," said the big man.

"I'm through fetchin' for you, brother," Alf told him

bleakly. "If you want that knife you can unload the gold and dive for it yourself. If you want to kill me, that's all right too; one way or another, I won't be any longer dead." The big man glowered, and seemed to be debating. At the last he said, "All right, have it your own way for once. Leave the knife stay. Only thing I'd need it for's to kill you with—and you ain't worth killin'. Like I always said, a good big man's better'n a good little man every time; and you ain't even a good little man. You got brains for plannin', but no nerve for pushin' things through to the finish. So long, runt. I'll be thinkin' about you when I spend your gold."

Alf watched the big man move away into the gray vastness of snow and sky. Oddly, there was no despair in his eyes as he watched; only serenity now. He turned aside and crab-clambered through the drifted snow to the place where he had thrown the knife. He fished around until he recovered it.

Inside the cave again he built up the fire, warmed himself and rested. Then by the light of the smoky flames he poked around, exploring. He found two old discarded marrow bones, and a few leaves of tea which he picked up from the floor a leaf at a time. He cracked the bones, put them to boil with the tea in the shallow gold pan.

Then he went to work with the knife, taking one of the wolfhide coverings from the door and cutting it into thin strips. He unearthed a fox skin which he had spotted the first time he had entered the cave. It was drying on a makeshift stretching board, a crude contraption of bent willow withes. He took the willow withes, along with a few more which had been laced into the wolfhides to hold the door coverings in place, and sat down with them near the fire.

He worked purposefully, but without haste, first steaming both the willow sticks and the stiff wolfhide to make them more pliable, then painstakingly using them in fashioning something which would pass for a little man's snowshoes. At intervals while he worked, he drank of the bone and tea broth. Before he left the cave on his patchwork snowshoes—with the knife ready at hand—he fortified himself against the outside cold by sucking out what remained of the marrow in the bones; and he ate the soaked tea leaves. Such scant nourishment, he knew, wouldn't get him much farther than the make-shift snowshoes would. But he nursed a hunch that that would be far enough.

He didn't miss it. The tracks he followed through the still sub-Arctic twilight played out at last, as he had been so confident they would, and he came upon the big man's stiff and frozen body. It was half buried in snow, the bearded face gray with hoar frost. Alf sank down, dog weary, to rest on the big one's body.

No elation showed on Alf's hunger-pinched face, deep in the parka hood. Elation would come later—down in the warm country where there was enough of everything to eat for everybody, where men and women laughed, touching each other trustingly with their eyes, their words, their hands . . .

The gold? He'd carry the small pack only, come back next summer and look for the other. Maybe he'd find; there'd be a skeleton to mark the place. Right now it didn't matter.

Only the snowshoes were important. And food. He shucked his wool-gloved right hand from his mitt and took a firm grip on the handle of the long skinning knife.

For a last grim second, before using the knife, he contemplated the frozen hulk beneath him. Not any one thing, but a lot of little things all working together had brought the big one down. The whiskey which had exhilarated him enough so that for a while he hadn't felt the drain on his strength. It hadn't made him drunk. But it had made him much too scornful of the snow that clogged the deep-sinking webs, and the weight that rode his back as he drove for his goal: life—and a place to spend 90 pounds of gold.

And when the stimulant had worn off and fatigue had knifed in, as had been clearly evidenced by the shortening and wabbling of his tracks in the snow, his own great greed had prodded him further to extend himself. He didn't want to abandon the gold on the snow, because he could never be sure of coming back and finding it again.

Finally he had sunk down here and tried to unharness himself from the packs. There was nothing about the lashings that a man under ordinary conditions couldn't have mastered. But maybe he had recalled that Alf had helped to secure the straps. He might have remembered, too, Alf's last words, "I gave you your chance. . . ." Fatigued and panicky, the big man had fought the pack, as was shown clearly by the snow.

Finally he had thought of his knife. He could cut the straps! But the knife, of course, wasn't there. Quite possibly then he had quieted down, determining to rest and eat, then with renewed strength make short work of unloading the gold. He had reached for his food bag. And then he must have gone stark raving wild.

His bare hands showed it—bare hands in the 40-below cold! He had jerked his hands free from moosehide and wool to claw with his nails at the tough canvas of the food bag. And there was blood crusted around his mouth to show how, futilely, he had torn at the bag with his teeth.

And all the time the cold needling in, petrifying his hands, and soon thereafter his whole great body.

Alf shifted his mordant glance to the unopened food bag still clutched in the dead hands. The bag was a formidable looking object all right, the opening guarded by a knot twice pulled by the big fellow and afterwards wet with water by Alf himself.

The water had frozen, of course, glazing the knot with ice. Alf couldn't have untied it in a month of Sundays. But, of course, he didn't need to untie it. That was what he had the knife for.

The West's Number-One

Problem

A MAN WITH A nickeled law badge on his leather vest watched incuriously from the ferryman's tar-paper shack while Hally's wagon came off the landing apron. The wagon rocked with sodden creakings as Hally led the mules to the tie-rail askew between muddy snags of willows.

He had some time to kill. He had to wait for the ferry to go butting back across the Mississippi for Jake and the other wagon. Excitement needled him softly as his eyes traced out the road that wound off across the Illinois flood bottoms to the bluffs, blue in the miasmic autumn haze.

Lincoln's country!

That was how Hally Harper, of Texas, had always thought of it up north here—Abe Lincoln's country. In Texas the War Between the States had never really touched them closely. No invading army had raked them up and down. Some blood had been spilled, but it hadn't wet down Texas land; and no barns had been burned. Hally had been much too young for the war anyway, so that now, ten years afterwards, standing on Lincoln's land, there was no bitterness in his heart—just this excitement as he breathed in the alien air of the great gray river, air so thick with earthy essence that to a dry-land man it was like inhaling frogs and fish and mud.

His lank body bent, and his hand scooped up some of

the caked river loess. He examined the dirt with critical interest, held it to his nose to smell, let it dribble away between rolling fingers. While his hand dusted itself against travel-worn jeans, his hungry eyes kept looking. So this was the black dirt country, where corn grew tall and hogs grew round with fat, the place which—according to Little Bit Ewing's father, who should know—was destined to become the market feeder for all the cows in Texas.

Thinking of Little Bit's father, of course, made him think of Little Bit. And thinking of Little Bit pulled at him inside somewhere, made him feel sad and lonesome and very far from home. Little Bit was only seventeen, three years younger than himself, but the way she talked at him, with that grown-up woman seriousness, made him feel younger than *she* was sometimes. Little Bit had blond hair that was natural-curly, and the same tawny-smooth color, he'd bet, as this Illinois corn when it was silking out.

It was because of her that he was here, so he could prove to her good and plenty that he had reformed, and become the kind of man a girl could depend on, a good provider. Money had never interested him a nickel's worth. Not till now. He just liked to be figuring on things, new things, and working to make things grow.

But Little Bit had shown him how wrong that was. It was downright scan'lous, she averred, the way he went around all the time with his head in the clouds and let people take advantage of him. It wasn't as if he wasn't smart. She'd point out that he had been almost the first one to foresee that fencing was going to be the West's number-one problem. He hadn't let her tough-hided father or anyone else talk him out of that notion.

"The open range is doomed," he had indelicately informed Little Bit's father, who was one of the real old-time cowmen. "With these new railroads reachin' out onto the plains, bringin' in more and more settlers, dry-land farmin's the order of the day. And farmin' and ranchin' can't abide side by each—not without proper fences—"

"Proper fences, there's the catch," Little Bit's father had pounced upon him. "Here on the plains there ain't no proper fences. Too expensive to haul in plank and rail all the way from timber country. Government statistics show that fences out here cost more'n the stuff they inclose—"

"Sure," Hally pounced back. "That's why the West's been so slow to grow. No proper fences. But now there is one. Hedge—"

"Hedge!" The vast contempt of the open-range man was in the word. "Hedge! I've seen it all. Shanghai, bloomer, mesquite, Cherokee rose. . . . I've even heard 'em advocate, serious, prickly pear. But there's somethin' the matter with all of 'em. Either it costs out of sight to grow, or takes too long, or it spreads all over creation, or the stock butts through it, or *eats* it—"

"I didn't say just any kind of hedge, Mr. Ewing. One special hedge. Osage orange."

"You meanin' bois d'arc, young Harper, like grows wild all up and down the cricks? What the Indians used to make their bows from?"

"The same, Mr. Ewing. Full grown, it won't cost hardly fifty cents a rod. Four years after planting it'll make a thorny wall, as a fella says, that's pig-tight, horse-high, bull-strong. Yes sir, Mr. Ewing, osage orange is the answer to the fencin' problem."

Mr. Ewing disposed of the argument by saying flatly, "I haven't got any fencin' problem, young Harper."

But Hally hadn't let him get away with that. "Time's

quick coming when you will, sir," he had sounded dire warning.

It certainly wasn't very bright of Hally, Little Bit had pointed out severely, for him to cross her father this way— not when Hally pretended to love her father's daughter so much.

Pretended! When it was making him sick, he loved her so much! But she'd fall in love with him all over again. She'd drop Jake like a hot pancake when they got back to Texas again, and flashed the profits of this wagon trip on her. Four thousand and eight hundred dollars. That's the way this boom Illinois market was going to pay off on what he was wheeling in the two wagons. Little Bit would see then what kind of a provider he'd be.

Oh, this *pasear* into the corn country was going to fix everything fine for everybody! Even Jake, one way of looking at it. Because Little Bit had never been Jake's girl anyway, not rightly speaking. So he wouldn't miss her for very long. It might even be a relief to him, because the main thing Jake liked to do was make money, and with Little Bit out of his life he'd have more time for making it, because Little Bit was the kind of girl who took an awful lot of a man's time—

"You hard o' hearin', bub?"

It wasn't so much the voice that snapped Hally out of his daydreaming, as the sun glinting in his eyes from the nickeled law badge. The man himself was the one who had been standing in the doorway of the ferryman's shack when Hally drove off the ferry. Little and mild looking, he carried a day's growth of gray stubble on his leathery face. From under a shapeless felt hat his blue eyes looked out, mild too, but somehow sharp at the same time, not missing anything.

Hally stirred, blinked. "I can hear all right."

The lips warped into a slow grin, showing tobacco-stained teeth. "I spoke twice and you never budged. I dunno what, exceptin' a woman, could put a man out of the world thataway."

Hally's face turned a brick red. He clamped his lean jaws tight and looked away, trying to think of something man-of-the-world to answer. His glance was held by the hedge straggling back over the bottom land from river's edge. Leafless now, its thorny branches were limned against the autumn sky. Cornstalks and other flood debris clogged the hedge on the up-current side, and where the water had undercut, the orange-yellow roots, like exotic snakes, were tangled.

Hally's head jerked to indicate the hedge. "Always heard as how this was uncommon good country for osage."

The marshal nodded. "That what you wheellin'? Seed?"

"Yeah. Osage orange seed. Sixty bushel. Thirty on this wagon, and thirty comin' across on the next ferry." In his mind he made some more arithmetic. At $80 a bushel on the Illinois market, or thereabouts—eighty times sixty: $4,800! And that was enough for a Texas boy to get married on.

The lawman was watching him, and now with the same elaborate casualness a man down home might have shown in questioning a stranger, he said, "Texas, I'm guessin', judgin' from the down-country hat."

"Texas, yeah."

"Think o' that. All the way from Texas with seed."

"The close corner of Texas, Fannin County on Bois D'Arc crick."

The lawman's next words seemed to Hally to be framed with a casualness wholly unneedful.

"What's seed sellin' at down there?"

"Twenty dollars when I left." Hally felt suddenly uneasy before the other's mild stare, and he didn't know why.

The marshal busied himself rolling a cigarette. When the pause began to be awkward, Hally said, "With a boom market like what you've got here, I reckon she fluctuates a little every day." He paused as he realized that unconsciously he was matching the other's over-casualness of tone. He made himself ask the question directly.

"What's it sellin' at here?"

The marshal put a match flame to his brown paper cigarette, and looked away over the drab bottomlands.

"Twenty dollars," he said.

Out on the river the crawling ferryboat exchanged toots with a St. Louis packet. Overhead a crow flapped lazily, cawing.

Hally blurted, "Reckon I didn't hear you right."

"You heard me, bub. Twenty dollars."

Hally tried to tell himself that he had sensed what was building up from the second the marshal got so careful in his talk. But he hadn't sensed it, and the shock was on his face.

"Twenty dollars," he made dazed talk. "I could have got that much back home. From eighty to twenty—I don't see how, even in a runaway market—Why, I read it in the paper myself. The Galveston News. Eighty dollars on the Peoria, Illinois, market—"

The marshal was shaking his head. "I been takin' little fliers in seed myself, same as everybody else around here. Couple of years ago we went osage-orange crazy. Seed nosed up to eighty dollars a bushel. It ain't been anywheres near that since. Here the last couple months it's been up and down from twenty."

"Mister, I'm tellin' you I read it in the papers myself—"

The marshal let smoke seep, thin and blue, from between his lips. "Somebody bring you the paper maybe to
read, bub?"

"Why yeah—my friend that's comin' across on the next
trip of the ferry with our other load."

"You see the date plain?"

"Plain as the nose on your face."

"Was it on the outside of the paper, or on the inside
where the market reports was?"

"Why, on the outside—and the inside too, I reckon—"

"You reckon. But you ain't sure? Think hard."

"No, I ain't sure. Not exactly. But I saw the date on
the outside, and my friend brought me the paper. Why,
we're in this together—In a way, we are. Why, you're not
meanin'—"

"You been bounced, bub," the marshal said dryly.

Hally stared helplessly.

"It's a trick I heard tell of before," the marshal said.
"Somebody shows you the paper. The date's all right on
the outside where you see it big and it makes an impression. But on the inside where it counts, it's smudged or
tore off, or even doctored if the bunco man is sharp
enough."

"But this was my friend!"

"Sure. They always are."

Hally was fumbling in the pocket of his blanket-lined
jacket. He yanked out a folded legal document. "I—there
must be some mistake somewhere. I've got a contract—"

The marshal looked it over. "Humm," he said. "Humm.
This friend of yours, this party of the second part, this
Jake Cole, he furnishes the teams and wagons, huh, his
time and labor, at the fixed charge mentioned here?"

Hally nodded. "That's Jake's main business—freightin'."

"But the equity to the entire sixty bushels remains with you?"

"That's right. I'm a professional hedge grower. It's my seed—"

The marshal handed back the contract. "Bub, you don't own one solitary seed of that sixty bushels. Time it's sold off at twenty dollars and you pay your freightin' bill to this party of the second part you won't have a red cent left. You might even be owin' a little. You could likely save yourself money by abandoning the wagons here and now, turnin' around and headin' for home."

Hally just stared, his throat dry and tight. And they started coming back to him now—the damning little details of their wagon trip across the wild humped hills of Arkansas and the tail of Missouri, that put the guilt squarely to Jake Cole.

That lawyer friend of Jake's in Paris, Lamar County, next to Fannin—Jake had insisted on making everything legal on paper. For Hally's own protection, Jake had explained. But after that first stop they'd stayed on the back roads and never rested over at any towns. Jake had made the trip before, and he would always know a shortcut that took them around the towns. And twice when it looked as though they'd inevitably be spending the night at a town, Jake had had something go the matter with his wagon, so that they'd stopped to fix it, and then driven through the towns at night to make up for lost time.

All this just so Hally wouldn't get a chance to talk to anybody who might have some honest quotations on the osage orange market. There was even the time they found the Kansas City newspaper. But Jake made sure he had the first look at it—and by the time Hally got it, the market sheet was missing.

Oh, Jake had been slick all right. Starting from the very first when he had come fawning with his proposition.

"Sure set you up pretty with Little Bit, now wouldn't it, if you rolled home with a hat full of money that you got by shrewd dealin' up North—"

"What's Little Bit got to do with it?" Hally had flared.

"You and her—"

"Not anymore." Jake's voice sounded real sad. Everybody, when they first met Jake, thought he looked a little funny. He was big, with a red beefy face, but his eyes and mouth were little. The face looked too big for the eyes and mouth, or the eyes and mouth looked too little for the face. Something anyway. Everybody noticed it. But that was only at first. After you got to know him he looked all right, the same as anyone else.

"What you meanin', not anymore?"

Jake shook his head, looking dolefully sincere, with his little eyes and little mouth screwed up so tight they were almost buried in his chunky face. "Be honest with you, Hally," he said confidentially. "I figured I could make the grade for a while. But Little Bit, she's got you in the bottom of her heart. Only thing is, she says you never could make enough money to head up a family, that you're goin' to be all your life wastin' your time experimentin'—"

"Yeah, I know," Hally cut him off.

His experimenting had been a particularly sore point with Little Bit. She took the position that he was always trying to find a new way of doing something, when the old way was perfectly all right. Like about trying to improve on osage orange fence.

Hally had taken over Lafe Clendenning's droopy nursery stock, worked and fussed with it until he had the finest glossy green grove, with the closest growing branches and the most thorns of any in Fannin County.

He even figured out a way of separating the seed from the sticky pulp of the hedge oranges, by forcing the milled pulp through a kind of sluice box with holes bored in the bottom. His seed came out so clean he only had to wash it through two waters, and he got better than a bushel of seed from a thousand hedge oranges.

But after he had a good thing in osage orange, was he satisfied with that? Oh no, not Hally. He had to start experimenting then about a different kind of fence, a brand-new kind with wire, that hadn't even been invented yet. Hally was trying to invent it. *Invent something to put him out of his own business!*

"But, Bitty, osage orange ain't as perfect as I thought. Hedge just ain't the answer to the West's number-one problem. Shades too much ground for one thing. And there ought to be a fence, cheap like hedge, but that you could put up in the twinklin' of an eye almost, instead of waitin' four years for it to grow."

"And while you putter," she said bitterly, "we wait *twenty* years before we can get married, is that it? You keep saying when are we going to—but how can we, ever, Hally? You won't come down to earth long enough to even make a decent living for one, let alone two. It's not as though you couldn't. You—you're the smartest man I know—in a way. You predicted about the doom of the open range and about fencing being the West's number-one problem, and all, and—I love you, I love you! But you just don't care."

This last was said with tears and it made Hally feel awful. He felt still more awful when Little Bit went to the next schoolhouse dance with Jake Cole, who, whatever else they said about him, was a shrewd dealer and was putting his money by.

Hally didn't do anything about it except sulk, and the upshot was that Little Bit started going to *all* the dances with Jake Cole, and inviting him out to her father's ranchhouse for dinner Sundays.

Now on the bank of the river, Hally became aware of the marshal's intent look, and of his own hand involuntarily balled into a fist, smoothing itself against the palm of his other hand. "I am looking forward," he said gently, and more to himself than to the marshal, "to seeing Jake lead his mules off the ferryboat."

The marshal's troubled eyes held on him. "Now don't you be gettin' ideas too big for your Texas hat, bub. You been buncoed—but legal. This ain't cow country you're in now. We got law here."

"What kind of law is it," Hally wondered bleakly, "that helps a bunco?"

"Right or wrong, it's the kind we got. You'd be surprised how most of my trouble nowadays comes from your plains fellas makin' the river crossin' here. Gettin' so's I might's well set up office in Homer's ferryboat shack." He paused, frowned. "You packin' a gun?"

"No," Hally told him. "I won't need no gun. I whaled the daylights out of him when we were kids. Reckon I can do it again."

Hally went and sat down in the dirt by the river where the ferryboat would land, and by the minute as he sat waiting he got less dazed, less hurt, more purposefully angry. His eyes stared hard and bright as the steam ferry came hammering closer and closer, smudging its yellow smoke across the back trail made by the stern wheel spanking the muddy water. When the boat touched shore he didn't even wait for the wooden landing apron to be let down. His boots sloshed water and he climbed aboard, confronting Jake Cole there at the head of the mule team.

With Jake shying back, alarm in his round little eyes, quick knowledge and defiance in the set of his little mouth, Hally lambasted him:

"I know why you done it, Jake. You made money on me. But that wasn't all. You lied to me too—about Little Bit. You ain't through with her, like you said. You figured by this deal to discredit me more in her eyes than what I already am. You didn't aim to tell her about the two-year-old Galveston paper you sprung on me, did you? No. You'd just make out like it was my lame-brained idea to come up here and gamble on the seed market. You knew that without my seed money I'd have a hard time to carry over till next crop. You knew I'd have to sell somethin'—maybe my whole grove—"

Jake was still backing away, his big shoulders hunched, the little mouth working. "I don't know what you're talkin' about—"

"Seed," Hally enlightened him. "Twenty dollar seed! Been sellin' for twenty all along, the same here as at home. And good and well you knew it—"

"You locoed or what?"

"Jake, here it comes!"

Hally moved in with a Sunday punch calculated to knock Jake, big and beefy though he was, backwards off the ferry. But Jake had time to hunch his shoulders more. Hally's fist skidded from the blocky muscles and struck an indecisive glancing blow on Jake's cheek.

Jake covered up, backing against the mules, then clinched when Hally came tearing in again. Jake was bawling all the time. Things like: "Quit it, Hally! For Gawd's sake. What's gone the matter with you? I don't want to fight you. I ain't mad at nothin'. Quit it now—cut it out—"

Hally, mad all the way through, saved his breath for

his punches. In the clinch he strained and bucked, trying to break clear of Jake's bear hug, ramming at Jake—short-traveling blows that he knew, maddeningly, weren't hurting much because Jake was holding in too close.

Out of the tail of his eye he could see the ferryboat man and the marshal, interested spectators, edging closer. Jake started directing his pleading at the marshal: "Haul him offa me. I don't want to hurt him. He's my friend, but he's gone locoed. He don't know what he's doin'—"

Hally got in a shoving blow against the face that seemed to loosen Jake's hold. Hally could feel Jake's binding arms going lower, working down around the midriff, and hope bit Hally hard that there would be elbowroom pretty quick now for a haymaker, though in that same high moment of hope there was vague wonderment that Jake should be weakening so fast.

All at once there was a new quality about Jake's pleading voice, a panic-stricken note, and that was odd too because there was nothing about any of this to make Jake *that* much afraid. Hally glimpsed the little eyes under their sun-bleached brows popping with what seemed like stark terror. He still didn't get it, but the next moment he did, as Jake appealed pitiously to the marshal:

"Help me—the gun! He's going to kill! He's got a gun! In his pocket. He's tryin' to pull it out. I'm holdin' agin' it—but I can't—much longer. The gun—in his pocket—help me—"

From underneath the flapping leather vest the marshal drew his own gun from its snug hip holster and moved in fast. There was a gun in Hally's side coat pocket all right, just as Jake had said—a small derringer, a weapon vicious as a stub-tailed rattler.

The marshal in his way was merciful. When Hally

wouldn't quiet down, when he persisted like a wild man in going for Jake even in the face of the marshal's drawn gun, the marshal didn't strike with the heavy six-shooter barrel. He stepped in and dropped Hally with a single chopping blow of his fist—the fist weighted with the derringer he had lifted from Hally's own pocket.

Illinois jails, Hally took dismal note, were not much improvement on Texas ones. Though in Texas it was easier to stay on the outside of them. Maybe it was true, after all, what they said about the North—those diehards back home who were still fighting the Civil War ten years after it was over.

They said a southerner didn't have a chance in the North, that it was bossed by scallywag politicians who would throw you in jail just on general principles. *And keep you there!*

Jake Cole was anyhow halfway to blame for it though. Lower'n a snake in a wagon track—why, he hadn't known a Texas man had it in him to be so deceitful. And Little Bit—well, any girl who would go and take up with a man the stripe of Jake Cole—well. Jake could have her, and good riddance.

But there would come one fateful day when he rode back to Texas when he would stomp into Little Bit's no-account house that Jake would have built for her, and he would shove Little Bit to one side if she got in the way, and her children too—her red-faced, bug-eyed, fish-mouthed children—and then he would put his fist to Jake Cole the way he had meant to do today. Man, he would knock him clean through the plaster into the yard outside.

"Ain't he some pretty," he would say to Little Bit, and then he would stomp out again.

Maybe the next day he would go back and do the same thing again, because in Texas they didn't put he-men in jail for troddin' varmints.

He felt something nudging him. He stirred on the edge of the built-in wooden bunk, and lifted his head from cupped hands, looking up wearily. His frowsy cell mate, an old man, stubbled and shag-haired, drunk or crazy, maybe both, was staring at him with rheumy-eyed intensity.

"You hard o' hearin', younker? I been talkin' and you don't answer me none. Jus' rockin' and groanin'. You got the miseries?"

"I got 'em bad," Hally confided.

The oldster nodded sympathetically. "I dunno which is worst, miseries or stomach ache."

"Miseries is worst."

The old man pressed so close that Hally had to turn his head to miss the alcoholic breath. "Goin' to show you somethin' to cheer you up, younker." The old fellow's eyes took on a crafty look. "They think I'm crazy in this town, and every time I take a drink and get to feelin' my oats, like, they puttin' me in here. They're ignorant. They's destiny overshadowin' 'em and they don't know it. But you, younker, you got sense enough to recognize genius when you see it—and overshadowin' destiny. Ain't it the truth?"

Hally let him rant.

"You won't tell nobody, will you, what I'm about to show you?"

"I won't tell," Hally humored him.

Secretively, the old man stumped to the other bunk, lifted the corn-husk tick, and from beneath it took out something wrapped in a grimy flour sack. He brought it back to Hally.

"Always carry it with me," he said. He unwrapped it with slow and blundering hands, held it close for Hally to see. There was a new light in the oldster's eyes, a kind of slow fire; it might have been pride reflected there.

Hally looked at the strip of one-by-one board with nails driven through it every three inches so that the points protruded on the far side.

"What is it?" he asked helplessly.

"Overshadowin' destiny." The old man leaned close, whispered confidentially, "Folks comes and goes in this river town. Keelboats and packets. I talk to everybody. And what do I learn? I'll tell you. Since civilization has crept out from under the benevolent shade of forest trees and ventured out on the trackless plain, they is a problem overshadowin' the land. It is the West's number-one problem. It is the fencin' problem—"

Hally groaned, and rubbed his face with his hands, and looked at the old man through his fingers.

"The doom is on the open range," the old man went on. "Fences are the thing. But what kind of fences? You may well ask, younker, on account I am the prophet of the fences, unhonored here in Grand Tower. Now I will tell you what kind of fence. Not board, which is too expensive. Not hedge, which is pretty, and also useful for birds to build nests in, but which is slow to grow and troublesome to maintain. Not wire, which is too smooth, carryin' no authority with range critters. None of these things. But this!" He shoved close the board with the nails driven through it. "Wood married to wire. The answer to our number-one problem. Destiny—here in my hands."

"How does it work?" Hally asked politely.

"I am glad you asked. I'll tell you. You take a smooth wire fence, see? And you hang this board on the fence." He made exaggerated motions of hanging the wood on the fence. It didn't seem funny to Hally. But it didn't make any sense either.

His hand waved weakly out. "You just—hang it on the fence."

"All along wherever the fence goes. And whenever a beef critter takes a notion to leave for more greener pastures, and he starts to push through the fence, he feels the nails stickin' him and they determine him to stay at home. Wood and nails married to wire. The West needs a fence before it can grow. Here's the fence. Destiny!"

From the old man's trembling fingers Hally took the absurd piece of wood with the nails driven through it. Reflecting on some of the half-baked theories that he had spouted back home on the fencing question, he wondered, wryly, if he had sounded as crazy as this old codger. Maybe, he speculated, but for the grace of two-score years and a river of Monongahela whiskey, there stand I.

He couldn't help but think of the time Little Bit's father had brought in some wire to use for a corral fence. Johnny-on-the-spot with his sage predictions when the spools of wire were rolled down from the wagon at the Ewing ranch, Hally had said:

"Won't work."

Mr. Ewing took a tug on his cow-prong mustache and wanted to know why the hell not.

"Cows'll push right through it," Hally said. "Give 'em a few days to find out the wire won't hurt 'em—they'll push right through it. Needs somethin' they'll respect— like thorns."

"You would say that—you bein' in the hedge business," Mr. Ewing remarked dryly, and he went right ahead and strung his wire.

The next morning, early, Mr. Ewing came out and found Hally bending suspiciously over the new fence.

"What in the name o' Satan you doin', young Harper? If you're cuttin' my wire, I'll—"

"You know I wouldn't cut your wire, Mr. Ewing." Hally looked pained. "I'm tryin' to make an improvement on it, is all. When I got home last night I got me an idea—"

Mr. Ewing could see now that Hally had a bundle of osage orange switches on the ground beside him. There were some more switches that he had woven in and out between the wire of the fence.

"You call that an improvement?" Mr. Ewing kicked vigorously at the pattern of thorny switches between the wires.

Hally stood a little back, his long face maybe a little sad, his gray eyes certainly dreamy. "It seemed like a good idea when I got it. You see, Mr. Ewing, wire might be all right to send telegrams on, but it ain't the answer to the fencin' problem in the West. Wire's too smooth and delicate. The critters'll push right through it."

"I remember," Mr. Ewing said, "you were explainin' it to me yesterday."

The sarcasm didn't bother Hally. He said, still in his dream, "If I could think of somethin' to make the hedge switches stay in place better—some way to fasten 'em quick and cheap—But shucks, cut from the branch, them switches would weather too fast anyhow. Everything considered, Mr. Ewing, I don't think that hedge married to wire is the answer to the fencin' problem."

Mr. Ewing said, "Huh," in a very satisfied manner. "For once in my life, young Harper, I am findin' myself plumb in agreement with you."

But Mr. Ewing wasn't feeling so satisfied the next day. His new white-face bull that he had imported to build up his native stock, leaned against the smooth wire of the fence a couple of times, tentatively—then went through it as though it wasn't there.

Even Little Bit, by some kind of obscure feminine logic, seemed to hold Hally responsible for the bull going through the fence.

"If you'd just stick to your hedge," she said, "instead of dissipating your—your fine talents on trying to invent something to put you out of business even more than you already are—Really, honey—"

All at once Little Bit, Texas, osage orange hedge, even this Grand Tower jail, disappeared from Hally's awareness as though he had never heard of any of them. He had been staring at the dinky piece of wood with the nails in it, almost without seeing it. Now suddenly his hands started shaking worse than those of the old man, and he felt the flesh under his clothes prickling hot and cold.

There is a kind of thought that comes in a flash of lightning brilliance, whole-born and clean, and comes rarely in the lives of men. It is apt to be simple—and tremendous in its potentialities for changing the world as we know it. Such a thought, Hally dimly sensed, was this.

Like a man sleepwalking, he got up and moved across the splintery planks to the cell door. "Marshal!" he yelled. "Marshal!" He shook the bars of the door.

His voice was hoarse, and the old man looked after him strangely. "You feelin' a mite teched, younker?"

Hally kept up his racket until the marshal came from his office down the corridor from the jail cell.

"That won't get you nowhere, bub."

"Look, all I'm wantin' is some thin nails and a piece of wire, and a pair of pliers."

"What in the hell for?"

"I got an idea. I got to make somethin'."

The marshal of Grand Tower looked at Hally's knuckles showing white from the force with which he gripped the bars, he noted the way the sweat seeped out on his forehead, and he saw the light that was in his eyes, a kind of slow fire.

"Why sure, kid," he said quietly. "Sure. I guess it won't hurt none."

While the marshal looked on from beyond the barred door, and the old man squatted close with excited rubbering eyes, Hally worked feverishly with the pliers, bending the nails almost double and wedging them on the wire.

He held up his creation and talked, not to the marshal, but to the old man who would understand. "Not wood married to wire. But metal married to metal, see?"

"Aye, younker," the old man said. "But metal on metal won't hold in place." His grimy fingers poked out to move a bent nail on its wire axis. "Slips around no matter how you bend it. I tried it myself, long ago. It takes the wood to hold the metal prickler in place."

Hally's head nodded slowly. "You're right—the idea's no good." He could feel the life seep out of him, right out of his fingertips.

Then there it was again, unasked, unbidden—a brain nudge from the gods.

"Wait a minute!"

Hally took the pliers and commenced cutting the wire in foot lengths. He stopped with half a dozen and fastened the lengths together in a kind of chain, but putting a half-inch crimp in the end of each length and coupling one to another.

"Now we'll turn the crimped ends out a little to each

side." He made the adjustment with the pliers, and held up his wire chain. "Now what have we got? Thorn-wire—but without the wood!"

He stretched the wire chain tighter and tighter between his two hands. It broke at its weakest link—and Hally's spirits broke with it.

The old man wagged his head sympathetically. "It ain't practical. It'd be always breakin' somewheres. You need the wood. Like I showed you. I've tried every other way. And I ain't the only one. Up the north part of the state, De Kalb and Linckley and Kankakee and them places, everybody's workin' on it. They trot 'em out at their county fairs, the fandaglest things, and none of 'em works like my wood an' wire."

Hally's hands lay limply before him where he squatted on the floor. "Thought sure I had it that time," he muttered. "But I reckon wire just ain't the answer."

He didn't realize what he was doing at first. Unwilled, unnoticed, his hands were moving, twisting one of the soft lengths of wire around and around another one. Then he saw what he had, and he felt the first faint nudging of that power that was maybe clear outside of himself, outside of his mind at least, his conscious mind—and then it was there again, that lightning of the gods, striking a third time in almost the same place, consuming him in a flash of clairvoyance that left his fingers nerveless, his body hot and cold.

His lips moved. "Wire," he murmured, "*is* the answer. Only not just *one* wire. It takes two. Two wires twisted, for strength, and to hold the prickers in place. Here's what I mean; I'll show you."

He grabbed up the remaining long length of wire and looped it around one of the jail bars. Then he took an end in each hand and started twisting one wire around another until he had a double-strand wire.

"And we'll use, not bent nails," he said excitedly, "but other little pieces of wire for the thorns or prickers. Cut 'em on an angle to get the points." He demonstrated with the cutting pliers. "Later I'll figure on a machine to do it quicker. . . . Now we force the prickers in between the twists on the doubled wire, see, and bend 'em north and south so they don't slip out. The twists in the main wires will keep the prickers from turning. We got it! The fence the plains country needed! Smooth wire wasn't enough. But smooth wire doubled, twisted, and armed with wire thorns—"

"Destiny!" the old man's awed mutter sounded. "Like I propheted all my long life—only without the wood."

Hally went to the door, gripped the bars and talked through them to the marshal. "I got to get out of here—sudden."

The lawman shook his head, frowning. "She's out of my hands, bub. Your partner's swore out a warrant agin' you, legal, chargin' intent to kill and attack with a deadly weapon. That's serious. You got to be bound over for the grand jury, to stand trial—"

"But I got work to do!" Hally said furiously.

"That's never no mind to me, bub. Your partner said you get kill-crazy sometimes, that there's bad blood in you, that you was packin' that derringer and threatenin' him with it all the way up from Texas—"

"He lied! I never even knowed that gun was in my pocket. When he was clinched with me in the fight he put it in my pocket a'purpose so's he could get you to arrest me—"

"That's what you told me before. In the law business

you find out nearly everybody's got his alibi for everything." The marshal started moving away. "Anyhow, I
don't make the laws; I'm only paid to enforce 'em."

Hally fumed and shook the door—then quieted down and
went back to his creating, perfecting the crude idea which
he knew with surety was the answer to all his fence experimenting. He decided it would be most efficient to bend
up a batch of the double-pronged wire thorns separately.
He could even figure out halfway how to do it. Use something with a moving shaft, something—well, like a coffee
grinder. Put a couple of pins in the end of the shaft, turn
the hand and feed the wire between the moving pins. The
wire would coil around the pins, and some kind of cutting
attachment could be rigged up to cut off the completed
wire thorns. It could be a continuous process. Sure. Then
string the coiled thorns on a long piece of wire and twist
another wire around it, leaving a wire thorn every few
inches between the twists. Nothing to it!

But first he had to get out of this damn' jail! It was
very depressing. Here he could solve the West's number-
one problem and he couldn't figure out a simple thing like
how to get out of a locked room. He brooded on that until
nightfall when the marshal came bringing their supper:
fried young rabbit and mashed potatoes with rabbit gravy,
big slabs of white bread with butter and sorghum, pickled
peaches, and coffee with rich cream and sugar in it, all
prepared by the marshal's wife.

The marshal stuck around and watched them eat.
Afterwards he unlocked the cell door and jerked his head
at the old man. "All right, Wood'n-wire; I guess you're
pretty near sober."

Before the old man went out, he paused in the yellow
light that sifted down from the wall lamp in the corridor

and gripped Hally's hand with both his own. "Here," he
said. He presented Hally with the dirt-glazed flour sack
containing the strip of wood with the nails driven through
it. "I want you to have it, younker. Makes me feel kind of
clean somehow—like when you give up idols and false gods
when you get the true religion. You've showed me the gos-
pel way about fencin'. It ain't wood married to wire. It's
smooth wire twisted double and pronged with more wire."

After the old man had stumped out, the marshal said
quietly, "It's dark enough now. Give me five minutes or
so to get to the other end of town, then try the door. Should
you find it unlocked, bub, leave your conscience guide
you. And if I was from Texas and lookin' for a man with
sixty bushels of osage, I wouldn't go to Peoria. I'd take
the North Pike out from town and head for Murphysboro.
Leastways there was a lad in this town hired today to drive
a Texas wagon there. And it sounds reasonable to me on
account Murphysboro's a sight closer to here than Peoria,
with the seed market about the same."

Hally blinked incredulously in the yellow light. "You
mean you—you'd do that for me—"

"I don't guess there's any local taxpayers as would
object—"

"But the law—"

"Maybe it ain't so much different here than in Texas,
bub. The law gets to workin' an injustice, and straight-
away a man starts figurin' how to get around it. I wasn't
sure about you this mornin', but now I made up my
mind."

"Gee—why, well, thanks, Marshal—shucks—"

"That wire you twisted up today—you think you really
got somethin' there?"

"Marshal," Hally said warmly, "that hank of wire
sounds the death knell of the open range. Likewise the

hedge business. I predict that two short years from now, there won't be another professional hedge grower in the United States."

The marshal grinned. "A fella'd better start tradin' short then on osage orange seed, hadn't he?"

"I reckon," Hally said, but with less enthusiasm, recalling all of a sudden that hedge growing was his business.

Hally stayed on the road all night, and with the help of a lift part way in a doctor's buggy, he was in Murphysboro the next morning. He scouted around, and at Shivley and Neeson's Livery Stable he located Jake's mules and the two wagons still loaded with osage orange seed. He washed up and got breakfast at the Little Gem Cafe on the Court House Square. He still looked pretty grubby in his travel-worn clothes. But there was no help for that. He inquired around and went to see a lawyer.

J. Worthington Plunket at his rolltop desk, in his wing collar and black string tie and black coat, and with his white fingers that kept lacing while the thumbs twirled, was not so much different, Hally observed, from Texas lawyers. Hally explained about the osage orange seed.

J. Plunket, attorney at law, looked at the contract and gave his dry and measured opinion. The party of the second part, he opined, could indubitably secure a court attachment on the seed and prevent Hally from selling until the freighting bill was paid. Hally would be indeed fortunate, he said, if he had enough money left with which to pay his lawyer for this consultation.

"All right," Hally said, "that's how I thought it was anyhow. It don't matter. The hedge business is doomed anyhow. Here's the main thing I wanted to see you about."

From out of the old man's flour sack he lifted a sample length of pronged and twisted wire. He waited expectantly for the glow of interest to show in the lawyer's eyes.

J. Worthington Plunket merely looked bored, even a little annoyed.

"It's a new kind of fence," Hally enlightened.

J. Plunket's thumbs twirled. "So?"

"I invented it—me and an old man in jail—I mean in—in another town. I want the papers drawn so he gets his share of the profits."

The lawyer continued to stare. And now there was no doubt of it; the expression on his pursed lips was one of annoyance.

"I want to get it patented," Hally persisted.

The lawyer tilted forward in his swivel chair. "Young man," he said severely, "we have jails in this state for those who infringe upon patent rights."

Hally looked a little dazed.

The lawyer further elucidated. "The whole top half of this state has been racing for the patent office this summer. There must be by this time fifty patents issued or pending for this"—his white hand waved out—"barbed wire. Why there is even a man in this very township manufacturing some of it under a royalty arrangement with a patent holder from De Kalb. And now, young man, if you will excuse me"—the swivel chair turned back to face the rolltop—"my time is valuable."

Still dazed, Hally found himself outside the door. He almost bumped into Jake Cole without seeing him as Jake turned the corner on the square-brick sidewalk and approached J. Worthington Plunket's office. Jake was the first to get his voice. His little eyes bulged like peeled grapes, and his little mouth kept opening and shutting.

"Hey," he blurted, "I thought—How'd you get—"

"I shot the marshal and burned the jail down," Hally told him. "And it ain't half what I'm goin' to do to you."

He would have swung then, regardless of Illinois law, its jails, and its lawyers. But the door behind him creaked open. A suave voice said, "Ah, the party of the second part, I believe. Come in—come in—"

Jake went in right now, and the door snap-locked behind him. Hally moped away down the street. The autumn sun filtering through the bare branches of the maples did not warm him. Even the squat houses built of Bellville brick seemed to glare with hostile intent through their windowed eyes. Fannin County and Little Bit were a million miles away and this was the moon or somewhere. And he was sure sunk. He'd thrown a wide loop, and no chance now for another toss.

He did remember after a while about the lawyer mentioning a man in the township who was manufacturing what he had quaintly called barbed wire. There couldn't any good come of it, but now that he was here it wouldn't hurt to take a look. He inquired around and walked north from town on a rutted road bordered on both sides by osage orange hedge. Tall prairie grass, cured on the stem, swaddled the road clear to the wagon ruts. The wind made a mournful rustling in it.

Hally stopped at the first farmhouse with a white picket fence around the front yard. He turned in at the gate and followed the board walk around to the back. A young man, bareheaded and sun-kilned, and maybe a few years older than Hally, had his sleeves rolled up and was washing in a tin pan near the pump. He looked up and smiled, gray eyes frankly curious, as Hally came around the corner of the house.

"Thought I heard the gate squeak. Been meanin' to oil it. . . . Howdy, stranger."

Hally said howdy, and introduced himself as Hally Harper from Texas. "Was lookin' for Joe Trihey," he said, "who runs a—a barb-wire factory." He looked expressively around at the house and the cluster of farm buildings: summer kitchen, henhouse, plow shed, barns. "Reckon I've stove up against the wrong place."

The farmer reached for a towel, plunged his hands in the unbleached muslin, and rubbed vigorously. He hung the towel back on its wooden peg. "Nope, this is the right place, all right." He stuck out his damp brown hand. Hally took the hand and they shook. "Just sittin' down to dinner." He clapped Hally on the back. "You come on in and join us."

After the grief he'd been through, this was so much like the neighborly "light an' set" welcome he was used to at home that Hally felt a lump rising in his throat, and he turned and started pumping water strenuously to splash some water on his face before any tears might show.

Dinner was hearty and friendly, with the Mrs. in her blue print housedress continually jumping up to bring on hot, covered dishes from the kitchen, and hovering around them while they ate; and the three children kicking the legs of their chairs while they ogled the guest and giggled over their secret knowledge.

After dinner Joe took Hally out in back to the milk shed. He lifted the whittled peg on its leather strap and let the flimsy plank door swing wide. He waved Hally proudly inside.

"My fence factory," he said.

Hally looked about bewilderedly. Then, eyes focusing to

the dimness, excitement prickled him as he saw what was stacked in the corner: finished fencing wire wound loosely on big wooden spools—six spools of it, ferocious stuff with inch-long steel thorns, or barbs as they called them up here, daubed with red lead to keep them from rusting.

Hally caught his breath again as he saw the doctored-up coffee mill with the casing cut away and the two pins driven into the end of the shaft so that the barbs could be given the desired bend when the handle turned—just about the way he had pictured it back in the Grand Tower jail.

"Now come out in the yard," Joe invited, "and I'll show you how I twist the wire."

They stopped in front of the grindstone.

"That?"

"Sure. I grease the wire and carry one end of it to the top of the windmill. The kids climb up with a bucket full of barbs and string 'em on the wire, let 'em gravity-feed down. They think it's fun. Next we take two fifty-foot lengths of wire and hook 'em up on one end of the grind-stone. The kids turn the crank and I space the barbs between the wires as they start twinin' together. Result: a fence that shades no land, that's better'n hedge or boards—"

"You don't have to sell me!" Hally exclaimed. He stood looking, his expression rapt. "A coffee mill and a grind-stone—destiny in our hands."

"Course, the way I'm goin' at it," Joe apologized, "it ain't much more'n a hobby. I can't turn out the wire much faster'n I can use it here on my own place. But I think a mint of money could be made if a fella was to go after it serious-fashion. Folks around here think I'm cracked on the subject. But I claim barb-wire is the comin' fence in the West. I think the demand is goin' to exceed the supply for a while." His voice warmed with his enthusiasm. "What makes it so practical—it's a natural for machine production. There's patents already pendin' on machines the same principles as these of mine, only operated by steam, fast and cheap. You buy the smooth wire from Washburn and Moen in Massachusetts. Then make it into barbed wire and sell it. A man could make a mint of money. But shucks, it takes money to start a thing like that—money that I haven't got."

"How much money?" Hally asked tensely.

"I've figgered till I'm black in the face. I can't get it down below three thousand."

Hally took a long breath. "Joe, could you use a partner?"

"With three thousand dollars? You joshin'?"

"No, I'm not joshin'."

Their eyes caught, hung.

"You mean *you* got three thousand? Cash?"

"No, but I know where I can get it."

Hally's jaws set, grim as death, and Joe, watching him uncertainly, laughed shortly.

"You goin' to rob a bank? You know we got laws up here—"

"Oh, I've found out all about your laws, Joe. No, I'm not goin' to rob a bank. But I'll go get the money—right now."

Hally didn't go looking for Jake Cole. He just went to the livery stable and sat on a stool and leaned back against the end post of a box stall, and waited for Jake to come to him. It was along the middle of the afternoon when Jake showed up. When he saw Hally sitting there, whittling, apprehension—and calculation—chased themselves all over his beefsteak face again, with his little eyes narrowed, his little mouth pressed tightly.

"Now listen, I don't want to have any trouble with
you—"

"You ain't calculated to—much," Hally said. He got up
and came toward Jake slowly, the knife still in his hand.
He kept his voice low, not to scare Jake so much that he'd
turn and run. "I just want one thing from you, Jake.
Three thousand six-hundred dollars—that bein' the sum
I would of netted up here on the osage orange seed, ac-
cordin' to the way you presented it to me."

Jake kept backing away, his eyes on Hally's whittling
knife. "You'll get what's comin' to you, Hally," he said
shrilly. "You know you will. After you've paid me my right-
ful freightin' bill."

"Freightin' bill will swallow the whole thing, and good
and well you know it. But it ain't just the seed of the
osage oranges I'm talkin' about now. It's my whole grove.
I'm sellin' it to you unencumbered for $3,600 cash in
hand."

Jake stopped backing away. His eyes blinked in quick
speculation. "How come you're wantin' to sell all of a
sudden?"

"Why you think?" Hally flared. "You reckon I want to
go back and be the laughin' stock of Fannin County? After
the way you played me—"

"You mean you ain't aimin' to go back?"

"Not if I can sell that grove."

"What about Little Bit?"

"Little Bit Ewing," Hally said bitterly, "is out of my life
just like osage orange."

Jake tried not to look too satisfied. "You'd want cash,
huh?"

"Cash."

Jake appeared to consider. He said carefully. "I have
got pretty friendly with J. Worthington Plunket. We could

go to him now and he could fix up the papers. Yes, I think he would do it. We could sell the sixty bushel of seed and I could arrange for a transfer of additional money from my Kansas City account. Lawyer Plunket can introduce us at his bank here in town. There is just about time before closing."

"Let's go," Hally said.

J. Plunket handled the details. He was very efficient about it. The pink-cheeked cashier at the Murphysboro bank pushed the money under the bronzed grille, and Jake Cole took it and counted it out to Hally. It was all there—minus the lawyer's fee, which Jake explained it was the universal custom for the one who got the money to pay. If the fee seemed unduly large, that was because the transactions had been put through with undue haste, lawyers every-where commanding extra remuneration for transactions performed unduly.

It never entered Hally's head that Jake and the lawyer planned to split the fee between them. It didn't even occur to Hally that the fee was exorbitant. He had only two thoughts at the moment. One was of Little Bit Ewing who was now out of his life forever, and it was nostalgic and sad. The other was of Jake Cole, and it was immediate and pleasant.

Hally tucked his money in an inside pocket and care-fully buttoned his jacket. Then he treated them all to a display of Texas individuality; he rubbed his hands, and somewhat like a great humped cat he started stalking Jake Cole.

"I been waitin' too long for this," he said.

The shocked cashier and the lawyer stared helplessly, horrified not so much by what was obviously about to happen to Jake Cole as by the impropriety of it happening inside the cherrywood-finished and marble-slabbed Murphysboro bank.

Jake Cole was horrified too. But not about the improprieties. Just about what was going to happen to Jake Cole. He started backing away, making ineffectual fending motions with his big hands.

"Now look here, Hally; there's law up here—"

In the end he must have adjusted to the inevitable because he stopped, and then lunged forward, beating Hally to the punch with a fist swung like a scythe, wide and low, at the stomach.

Hally had just time to heel sideways and suck his middle in and let Jake's first scrape past—and practically let Jake knock himself out against a hungrily awaiting fist. Hard on the chin where he had intentioned it—a mule-kick punch that Hally felt clear to his elbow.

Jake didn't strike his head against the Ozark marble floor. That was because, heeling back, he rammed into J. Worthington Plunket. That worthy went down first, flaying the air with outreaching hands. He landed most undignifiedly, spread out on his own coattails, inadvertently cradling Jake's collapsing body in his lap.

It was all very satisfying. Hally straightened his jacket at the collar and strode out the door. The first thing he saw out there was a girl who looked almost more like Little Bit than Little Bit herself.

She was struggling down the street from the direction of the railroad depot, with a useless parasol, a hat box, and a vast carpetbag banging against her knees. Even her clothes were amazingly like Little Bit's, from the perky little piece of black velvet with Christmas-tree-looking ornaments sewed on one side of it, and which she wore for a hat, to the blue and orange tweed traveling suit pinching her almost in two in the middle, but making her look wonderful above and below.

"Little Bit!" Hally shouted, with all the restraint of a bawling Texas longhorn.

His heels broke echoes from the square bricks of the sidewalk as he ran. And then she was in his arms, her bags and boxes plumping about her, while Murphysboro business men and shoppers, startled and grinning, looked on from the doorways.

Little Bit was crying and talking all at the same time, and Hally, ecstatically piecing things together, learned that:

She never could stand that Jake Cole anyway, and only went with him to make Hally jealous, and to try to get him to have a little more sense of responsibility, but she was afraid she had laid it on too thick about him not making any money, and she didn't care if he ever made any money or not; she loved him just the way he was and wouldn't change him for the world—well, not much anyway; he was a precious, precious thing, and to prove it she had come all the way up here by stage and the Cairo and Fulton Railroad and some other railroads to tell him so, because she was afraid he might get discouraged and maybe never come back to Fannin County and to her, after the way Jake, the horrid, slippery, crawling thing, had tricked him about the price of osage orange seed in Illinois—

That was where Hally got his first dazed word in. "But how could you be knowin' about that, Bitty?"

"Well, I know Jake, don't I? And I could put two and two together. I could read in the paper what osage orange seed was selling for up here—about the same as at home.

Jake made you think it was a lot more, didn't he? But I
don't care, honey. I've brought enough money for us both
to get home on—"

"Why, Bitty; I don't need any money." Hally raked the
currency from his pocket. "I sold my grove to Jake.
There's thirty-six hundred dollars here—minus the lawyer's fee. Look!"

Hally himself was doing some double-distilled looking,
but not at the money. From the tail of his eye he could
see Jake Cole, standing disheveled and groggy, in front of
the bank. He was flanked by two men. One was the lawyer,
likewise disheveled. The other was a hard-bitten individual who wore a law badge. The lawyer and Jake were doing
the talking, and all three men were looking at Hally in a
manner hostile.

Little Bit had eyes only for the wad of money. "Oh,
oh," she wailed, "it's worse than I thought! Thirty-six
hundred! Your place is worth twice—"

"It won't be—not for long. Why, honey, I'd of been
cheatin' Jake if I'd charged him more. The way it was, I
only charged him what he'd guaranteed I'd make on the
seed deal. You see, what Jake don't know is: osage orange
is goin' plumb out, honey. Barb-wire's comin in. I'm goin'
to stay up north here and come in with it—"

She tugged at his arm. "Look, there's Jake now! Coming
this way. He looks mad, kind of. He's got two men with
him. They all look mad, and one of 'em's wearin' a
badge—"

"This is the law-riddenest country!" Hally sighed, and
moving his lanky body to conceal his actions from the
approaching three, he crammed the money into Little
Bit's two hands. He talked swiftly. "Put it out of sight
quick, honey. Then I tell you what to do: take the money

and give it to Joe Trihey—the first farmhouse on the road north from town with a white picket fence around it—"

"But Hally," she gasped, "I—I don't understand. Where—will you be?"

"Me? I'll be in jail again, honey. But you're not to worry, hear? I reckon with all the law they got up here, there ain't one that a man can't be married in jail. Anyhow, they don't anywhere keep manufacturers long in jail—"

"Hally Harper, are you going crazy—"

"Could be." He grinned down at her. "Crazy in love anyhow. And crazy rich maybe. Leastways we will be if barb-wire takes the place of hedge—"

"Honey, I don't understand anything," she broke in, "and I'm scared, and I—I don't like it up here. Let's go home, Hally—right now." Through wet lashes she smiled her persuasive best. "Why honey, you've got the—the West's number-one problem to solve, don't you remember?"

"I've plumb solved it," he told her, and pulled her close. "From now on you're my number-one problem."

He had just time for a quick sample of how he proposed to solve that one before he felt the hand of the law on his shoulder.

Wood on the Snow

WHEN THE WORST of the Arctic storm was over, Bill Sloan started trekking again. He was headed for the Keewatin Exploration Co.'s base on Desperation Inlet. It was the last place on earth he wanted to go. But he simply had to go somewhere or die. And there was no place else to go.

Bill was pretty well-spent. Though he carried only a light ruck sack and a prospector's pick, he weaved in the jerking bluster of the wind.

The night was cold, a damp bitter cold which slowed the blood and cut into the very bone marrow. Each fresh blast of air that blew in from the coast was turned into a frost-powdery fog when it struck the barren Canadian hills.

That fog, with the wan moonlight filtering through, was deceptive, treacherous. Bill had to keep throwing a moose-hide mitt ahead of him as he walked. The mitt made a blur of black against the snow. If the blur disappeared, he knew the mitt had gone over a ledge and he pulled it back by its *babiche* cord and cast in another direction. It was slow going. He talked to himself as he foundered along. Sometimes he fell, but he always managed to get up promptly.

Bill was a philosopher. He had always said that if it came to a showdown on the trail he knew what he would do. Death was like a lot of other things—the only way to beat it was to accept it.

One thing certain—Bill Sloan's carcass would never

be found folded stiff and cold in the snow, with the knees and elbows a raw bloody-black from crawling. No, brother! When the time came that he had to crawl, he'd do something else. He hadn't got down on his knees to life.

And he wouldn't get down on his knees to death!

He'd fight death to the last rattling breath, but when he couldn't stand on his feet any longer, he wouldn't crawl. It would be time for something else then. It would be time to dig his own grave and lie in it. If the time ever came when he had to die on the trail, he'd die with dignity.

He'd always been pretty much of a roughneck. There hadn't been a lot of dignity in his life. But he could die that way. Peacefully and with dignity. He'd never had what you would really call a home—a place of his own. But he'd have his own personal grave, Yes, brother! They might cheat him out of the best things of life; they couldn't cheat him out of a grave.

The trouble right now was the gnawing cold. A fellow could stand it while he moved along. There was food—caribou jerky and prunes. Exercise and food would keep blood circulating. Sure thing. But you had to rest once in a while. And when you rested, you needed a fire. Rest without fire in this mercury-congealing weather was a quick ticket to another world.

Yes, you had to have fire. And to have fire, you had to have wood. He didn't have wood, and there wasn't a chance he'd find any wood. There was everything else in these Northwest Territories. But this side the timber line, very little wood.

It was funny about this country. It had never been appreciated. A rolling rock-ribbed tundra vast as the ocean. So vast it staggered you to think about it. All the way from the Rocky Mountains clear across to Hudson's Bay. All the way from the sixtieth parallel of north latitude clear to the Arctic coast. The great lone land. For a couple of months out of the year, simmering in summer heat and swaddled under a blanket of gay-colored flowers—blue lupines, yellow Arctic poppies, white and red saxifrages. For the other ten months, frozen, grim, defiant. As raw a land as when the glaciers left it, gouging out a million lake beds and plowing off the top soil to carry along down into the States. Unknown—as new and as old to-day as then: The great lone land.

But one of these times it would be coming into its own. There was everything here. Five million caribou roaming the frozen plains. Or maybe fifty million—who was here to count them? Gold enough beneath the moss and lichens to pay off the European debt. Silver enough to provide breakfast plates for every one in the Dominion. Coal enough to operate every machine in the British Empire double-shift for a hundred years. Copper enough to pave a red and gleaming road from Montreal to Edmonton. Lead, zinc, iron, platinum—name it. You could find it here. Everything except wood.

There was a joker though. Wasn't there always? The joker was—everything was here all right, but try to find it. In a million square miles, with each mile a bleak-eyed, frozen-faced image of its neighbor, just try to find whatever it is you're looking for.

Ah, but he had found it! "Gold." All his life, looking for the yellow metal, and at last he'd found it! A whole half mile of outcropping gold-threaded quartz! He'd just stumbled onto it. That was the way with a lot of good things in this country. You didn't even have to drill for them. They outcropped, lay smiling up under the open sky, just waiting for the right man to come along and stumble over them. But wasn't that the way everywhere with the best things? You could work and plan and even pray—then maybe you'd stumble onto what you wanted and maybe you wouldn't.

Brother, oh, brother, it was cold! You noticed it more when you were older, too. Talk about stumbling—why couldn't he stumble over some wood? But that was the one thing you couldn't stumble over in this country. The scrawniest scrub willows would be miles and miles to the south. And he was headed north to the coast. He had to keep on north now. He was too far away from everywhere else.

Bill was farther away from the coast than he liked to think about, too. He tried not to think about it. He just kept slogging ahead. He had been on his legs a long while. Exposure and fatigue were wearing down his resistance. The cold was getting in. He fell oftener now. When he fell, his numbed reflexes were slower in getting him up.

He tried not to become alarmed over his weakened condition. He tried to think about the gold he had found— and lost. Oh, he'd lost it all right, there was no doubt about that. Nothing new about it either. Didn't he always lose everything? But he wasn't crabbing. It was the breaks. Such a little thing this time. Firewood. He was losing his gold through lack of a little wood.

No wood—no fire. No fire—no staying in this country during the long winter. But with the powerful Keewatin Exploration Co. maintaining a year-round base at Desperation Inlet, you *had* to winter on your claim if you wanted to keep it.

Like a pack of wolves, that's what they were. Wolves waiting for you to go down so they could jump your claim. "Assuming control of deserted property," they'd call it. Or something like that. Oh, they'd be legal about it all.

At least, they'd make it sound legal. Which was the same thing if you were the kind that lived by the wolf-pack law and had money to hire wolf-pack lawyers.

What made it really tough was knowing that in the beginning he'd had enough wood. During the open months he'd scoured the watercourses for a hundred miles south. He'd canoed back every piece of ground birch and scrub willow that he could find, and when the ice closed over the waterways, he had enough wood stored by to eke out the winter.

Then that pathetic band of Yellowknives dropping in on him. The Indians were way north of their regular grounds. They'd lost their dogs and *komatik* through the ice. They'd been wandering wild—hopeless, half-starved, freezing.

Well, what could you do? You couldn't let anybody freeze or starve.

When Bill loaded the Indians down with food and fire-wood, enough to last them to the far southern timber line, it left him with such a pitifully small amount of fuel that it was only a short time until he had to abandon his claim and strike for the coast. The Exploration Co.'s men at Desperation Inlet would trade him his life for his gold claim. It amounted to that.

Yes, Bill gave up all he had in the world to help out a ragged handful of needy Indians. Bread on the waters, they say. But it had never worked that way for Bill.

The storm caught him halfway to the coast. It was one of those periodic northwesterly gales which whine out of the polar sea and rake the rolling Canadian barrens like a scourge of shrapnel.

Bill really didn't have a chance. His sleeping bag blew away. He was unrolling his eiderdown bag, and a cyclonic burst of wind tore it out of his hands.

He blamed himself bitterly at first. Such an accident should never have happened to a trail-wise man. But the thing was, it had happened. Just another one of those things—like death—that you had to accept. The breaks.

Bill never did find the bag. The fog and the snow and the darkness tended to that. And while the wind was tumbling the bag across the frozen tundra in the far general direction of Hudson's Bay, he holed up in a shale cave and waited three days for the storm to blow itself out. He had to burn up his last stick of firewood to keep from freezing. Even so, he didn't have enough wood for a steady fire. He was considerably weakened by exposure when he started trekking again.

Before he had gone very far, the bleak suspicion clawed at his brain that it was more than a gold mine he had given up in the name of charity.

The suspicion grew as he reeled along, falling, getting up, falling again. When he fell three times within a distance of ten feet, he knew for sure.

He sat still for a long moment on the glazed snow that last time, his worn body swaying, stiff joints creaking, muscles numb as the frozen rock. He had been slogging along on sheer nerves. But even nerves fail.

He had some difficulty in unslinging his short-handled pick. Good old pick. It had been with him everywhere, outlasted all his partners. Sooner part with his compass than with the old pick. It had uncovered lots of pay dirt in its time. Yes, brother! There was one more job for the pick—one more job, then it could rest, too.

Bill was a philosopher. He had always said that if it came to a show-down on the trail he knew what he would do.

He started sinking his pick in the hard-crusted snow. It was funny. He couldn't feel the pick in his hands. He couldn't hear the noise it made. But he could see it chip-

ping up the snow crust—little spurts of white, glinting
through the cold fog. There wasn't much wind now. Just
this still, dead cold soaking through every pore in his
body. Long fine needles poking through every pore,
thrusting in farther and farther, trying so hard to pierce
his heart.

He kept on working till his pick struck bottom. It
wasn't far. He laid the pick down and scooped out some
of the loose ice and snow till he could see the dark ground
showing through. He cleared a shallow spot the size of his
two hands. Then he rested. Only for a moment. He could
literally feel the cold eating into his vitals whenever he
quit moving.

When he took up his pick again, he felt a dull surprise
at the weight of it. He hadn't remembered it was so heavy.

Lift—sink—lift—sink. Each motion took a separate
and supreme effort. But he kept picking away.

Soon, very soon now—Freezing wasn't so bad. Anyhow,
the worst of it was over. No more pain to it now. After he
had finished digging, he would just stretch out in his
grave—peacefully and with dignity—and go to sleep.

Already life seemed far away. Like something dreamed.
Places he'd been, things he'd done, friends he'd had,
women he'd known. He'd always lived on the fringe of
life, never quite fitting in anywhere, the good things beckoning just beyond his finger tips. The sweetness of life
turning bittersweet. Always, when he tasted, bittersweet.

But he had never quit fighting. Or hoping. This last
year he'd met a woman, storm-tossed like himself. A
woman mauled and beaten by life, but remaining clear-
eyed and hopeful, her spirit unbroken, her passion for
living—and loving—undimmed by the years.

She hadn't wanted him to come North this last time.
She had asked him to stay. No fuss, but on her face a
mute appeal.

"I'll be waiting for you," she said, when he went. Her voice was low and steady, no tears hung in her eyes, but she trembled against him in good-by and she turned her head the other way when he went out the door.

There had never been a woman waiting for him before. Not a woman like this one, with a promise in her smouldering eyes of life's sweetness—fresh sweetness never turning bittersweet.

If he could have held on here through the winter, he could have sold out to the Exploration Co. in the spring. Those wolves at Desperation Inlet wanted what he had. They were expecting him to come to them—beaten. But if he did not come to them, they would come to him in the spring. What they could not seize, they would buy. All he needed was fuel to carry him through the winter. He knew now, at last. After all these starveling years, he knew. Love, a home, children. It wasn't too late. But it was too late!

He laughed a little at that. He wanted love, peace, a place of his own. But the cards dealt him a grave! Well, all right, the grave then. The grave was a place of his own. But there'd be peace aplenty in it.

His last wish—granted. A place of his own and peace.

A funny thought came to him, and he laughed again. What if he should uncover another rich vein here? You just stumble onto things in this country—and every country. The good things of life—you just stumbled onto them. You could work and plan and even pray—Now when it was too late, now when he was digging his grave, what if he should stumble onto another outcrop of gold-threaded quartz? Wouldn't that be the world's prize laugh?

Bill didn't think very long about this joke. Another funny thought crowded it out of his mind. This was a bigger joke than the other, but it wasn't one that made him laugh.

The pick became more leaden with every stroke, and he had to work slower and slower. And there came a moment, very soon, when the slowing pick sank into the snow and stayed there. His arm muscles jerked and quivered, and the pick pulled out of the snow finally and flopped over and lay there.

And now he knew. It was no longer an appalling fear. He knew, and it was the bitterest knowledge that had come to him during a lifetime of bad breaks.

What he knew was this: He had waited too long, *he had not saved enough strength from the trail to finish digging his own grave!*

His last wish—refused. He had been cheated out of life; he was going to be cheated out of a grave. It wasn't much to ask of life—a grave.

His head slumped forward toward that pitifully small hole he had dug. The bottom of the shallow hole shone up at him, darkly mocking.

Suddenly his frost-rimmed eyes blinked wide. A tremor ran through his veins. It was like a tiny shock, all over him, everywhere, tingling the very ends of his fingers and toes. A stirring of life in a fast-dying body. In an almost dead shell, life asserting itself.

His hands gripped hard on the pick handle. He commenced to dig. Short, quick, desperate stabs of the pick. Not into the snow. Not the crusted snow this time. Into the bottom of that hole so darkly mocking! *Into the outcropping vein of coal which his grave-digging pick had uncovered!*

And presently he took his hunting knife and hacked off a piece of cloth from his parka, and whittled some slivers from the pick handle. He whittled stiffly. He had barely enough life in his fast-numbing hands to get the match lighted.

He crouched, hugging the smoky coal fire to him, feeling those icy needles pull out of his pores. Nerve ends shrieked. The pain was anguishing now. But it was sweet pain. It was the pain of newborn life.

He had dug into the snow looking for death and he had found life! Coal! Those Yellowknife Indians, poor freezing devils—he knew now how they must have felt when they stumbled across his place and he gave them wood. The breaks—you just stumbled onto things. Or did you? Bread on the water—wood on the snow? Well, maybe. Anyway, here was coal. He'd winter through.

Box-Car Buckaroos

HERE WE COME, gallopin' hell-fer-leather over the Blue Butte foothills, and Ed Tremper's posse not more'n a long rifle's shot behind.

Us three hustlin' hossmen is close-bunched. Leanin' into the wind and settin' his mustang like he is roped to the saddle, "Blazin' Daylights" Jones is pickin' the path. Joltin' close after him is myself, Johnny Jonquil, bald-headed Bar X puncher and plumb old enough to know better'n to have got mixed up in no such fracas as what this is.

Kickin' dust in the percession's rear is that brainy young cowpoke, "Schemer" McCan. Schemer is toppin' his pink-eyed albino bronc, Gladys. Inside Schemer's saddle bag is six thousands of bucks of good United States currency, which same has been honestly pirated by us from that old range tartar, Ed Tremper, the same that's leadin' the pursuin' posse.

In brief and to wit: Ed Tremper sold us ramblin' rannies the King Midas gold mine, which only is a gold mine in name only, producin' copious bats and mushrooms, but no gold.

Still in brief and jist as to wit: Schemer McCan schemed up a scheme and sold that combination bat-kennel and mushroom-spread back to Tremper fer twice what the old skulldugger had gouged us fer it in the first place. Then we lit out pronto with our six thousands of dollars, nosin' our hosses back toward the old Bar X, which is a long and lonesome way from this hostile Blue Butte country.

Ed Tremper, he sees almost immediate that we have outbatted and outmushroomed him, and he gathers up his lead-pushin' collection agency and comes hellin' after us.

Well, as Tremper's posse gits closer, the direction Blazin' Daylights is leadin' us gits rougher and rockier. Where we are ridin' is through a V-shaped valley with limestone walls r'arin' high on each side. As we nears the short end of the valley, Blazin' Daylights raises his reckless shape in the saddle to look ahead and see which is the best way to turn.

A frown forms quick on his handsome cowboy face. He has seen that there ain't any best way. There ain't even any worst way. There ain't any way! A deep railroad gulch with a freight train standin' in it, is cuttin' off escape.

Things is lookin' depressed! Rock walls on each side that even Schemer's famous albino bronc, Gladys, couldn't climb; a deep railroad cut in front with a train in it; and Tremper's lead-pushin' posse comin' up fast behind.

It is the kind of purty mess that Blazin' Daylights is all the time gittin' his podners into. Blazin' Daylights, he is a man of action. It is his constant custom to leap first, then look around, interested, to see what is he going to land on. Mostly it is somethin' kin to a beehive. It don't never teach him no lesson, though; he jist leaves it to sad-faced Schemer McCan to git him out of it.

Schemer is the brainiest cowpoke which ever roped steers on the Bar X or any other spread. In this special case, if it would of been lanky old long-faced Schemer that was ridin' in front, he never would of got hisself and podners into no sich trap. Schemer, out of his sleepy-lookin' eyes, he notices things.

He notices somethin' right now, by hoss-fly, that causes him to leap off Gladys sudden!

Blazin' Daylights, he acts too. He pulls his six-gun and turns vigorous in his saddle, ready to perforate the posse.

"No!" bellers Schemer, with what is fer him surprisin' insistence, because of he is usual so lazylike and mild-mannered. "This here is Ed Tremper's country, not ourn, you dang dim-wit! If we shoot up his posse, they'll hang us high as clouds, at the finish—— Besides, I have noticed somethin'. Gimme a hand, quick!"

He bends down and starts wrestlin' with some old discarded railroad ties which, even though they are almost buried in the sand, his sleepy-lookin' eyes has noticed. We git his idea, and we chip in pronto. The valley floor is about on a level with the box car roofs, and in lesser time than it takes to loop a lasso, we have rustled up the railroad ties and made us a bridge to the top of the freight train.

"After we git our hosses on top of the box car," Schemer explains, "we'll pull up the ties and make another bridge from the train to the other side of the gulch. Tremper and his collection agency, they can't foller, because there ain't no more ties."

Well, it sounded like a good idea at the time. And it was all right to start. All our hosses is good, steady mounts, and with Schemer's sure-footed little pink-eyed Gladys settin' the example, ours foller. We all git safe across on top the box car.

We can hear the hosses' hoofs of the pursuin' posse clatterin' closer as we bend to yank the ties over so's we can bridge 'em across to the other side of the gulch. Then we hear somethin' else. It is a depressin' sound. It is the train whistle whistlin'.

"That there," says Schemer, grittin' his teeth, gold ones and all, "is the highball. This train is goin' to start."

Which it sure did—immediate! Schemer, he knows his

highballs. From escortin' so many trainloads of steers to Omaha and Chicago, he has rubbed lots of elbows with conductors and brakemen. He knows all about trains like he knows barnyards.

Well, at this critical junction, with the train jerkin' and the hosses pitchin' on top the box car and the railroad ties all fallin' off into the bottom of the gulch, why, Ed Tremper and his posse come tearin' around a shoulder of rock. Old Man Tremper on that big black hoss of his, he opens fire, and the slugs from his single-action .45 fans the air past all three of us fleein' fugitives. Tremper's hirelin's starts blazin' bullets too, and whoops like all hound dogs does when they have about chased their prey to its final doom.

But they whooped too soon, them hound dogs. Our doom wasn't final. Not yet. There's a curve right close ahead, and the train is pickin' up speed, and it ain't only a handful of seconds till us box car buckaroos is being' pertected from enemy bullets by the high rock ridge.

The last thing we see before the ridge shuts off our vision, is old Ed Tremper pullin' up short on his big black hoss, with a onholy look comin' over his stubble-bearded face, like he was laffin' a nasty laff at our expense.

Schemer, he is a scholar of human nature. Little things like that laugh of Tremper's have a meanin' for him. Pronto, he's suspicious. He looks all around and ahead. And he sees it.

Blazin' Daylights and me, we see it too, and it makes our hair rare up so sudden it might-near pushes our sombreros off.

What we see is that our train is goin' into a tunnel!

"Hai yai!" yells Schemer like a Sioux Injin; and, jumpin' on his white-haired bronc, he digs in the spurs.

Gladys looks around out of her pink eyes in indignant

wonder. Then, seemin' to sense the special emergency, she clops dainty along the narrow runway atop the swayin' box car, and under Schemer's firm young hand takes the jump across to the car ahead. My mustang is started by Blazin' Daylight's frightened hoss bitin' it in one of the last quarters.

So here we come, us three box-car buckaroos, racin' our horses along the top of the train in a mad race with death. What we are racin' fer is a low gondola car which we can see up ahead and which mebbe has got sand in it; and it will shore be comfortin' if we can git to it afore the tunnel gits to us.

It is some race, all right. The canyon walls roars past on each side. Them box cars sways and bounces, and some of the cars is a little higher and some a little lower, so it is a harrowin' spectacle, the way the hosses run along that runway of death and leap from car to car.

The harrowin'est of all is about me. My hat goes with the wind, and a hot spark from the injine sticks to my bald spot. Providence was carin' fer me in a slipshod kind of way, though, because what if I had had a long beard, and the spark had got tangled in it, instead of landin' on one of my less flammable portions!

Schemer leads a little away from us, and he jumps Gladys safe down into the gondola, thereby savin' hisself from a languishin' death by bein' knocked off the top of a freight train on a hoss by a tunnel. The car is a good old load of sand, all right. I breathes easier.

Sand is a near-ideal thing to make a forced landin' in with a hoss. However, Gladys gits kind of bogged, and goes down violent on her knees, so that our leadin' box car buckaroo takes a header and polishes his face in the grit.

He has no more than started to spit sand and cuss

about it, calmly, than he sees everything has happened
for the best anyhow, because my hoss comes rocketin' off
the top of the box car and turns heels over in the identical
place Schemer would of been, if Gladys had not went down
on her knees and throwed him.

Well, that tunnel is so mouth-open close by now that
you can smell its smoky breath, and with Schemer and
me and our hosses spread all over the sand car, there
ain't hardly no clear space fer Blazin' Daylights to jump
into. He jumps regardless, and darkness masks the strug-
gles of men and beasts as the gondola swoops into the
tunnel.

Mebbe it is a good idea that darkness has drawed its
kindly curtain, because there is shore some onchristian
snortin' and cussin' goin' on while us six combatants, men
and beasts, gits ourselves ontangled.

"Quit chawin' on my neck," Blazin' Daylights is heard
to roar as good as he can with the sand fillin' his mouth.
"I ain't nobody's beefsteak, you blood-clawin' coyote!"

"Who's chawin' your neck? I ain't!" Schemer retorts.
"It must be Gladys. Or mebbe it is a sand flea," he points
out with humor. "*Ugh-phg*," he grunts, interruptin' himself and grabbin' hold of his stomach sudden in the dark.
"Quit kickin', you shadder-brained jackass!"

"Who's kickin'? I ain't!" Blazin' Daylights bellers with
evident satisfaction. "It must be little pink-eyed Gladys."

When the gondola comes out of the other end of the
tunnel and darkness is drawed back, the pitiful scene is
revealed. The hosses are caplunkin' around wild, except
Gladys, who is nosin' at somethin' in the sand. That little
albino bronc has got the same onruffled nerves as what
Schemer has. Brains, too. She's always noticin' little
things, jist like Schemer does.

"Where's Johnny?" Blazin' Daylights voices. "Hey,

ain't that his bald head stickin' up out of the sand with
Gladys lickin' it?"

They dig me out and shake me a little bit, and soon
I'm as good as ever.

"Well," says Blazin' Daylights, as the train clanks
along, goin' some slower now, "so far, so good. We have
still got our six thousands of dollars, which will let us buy
in on that little spread at Floatin' Rock Springs. We will
be cattle kings yet, and sit in our ranch house with
nothin' to do but smoke them kind of ceegars which cattle
kings smokes."

"Mebbe," says Schemer in his cautious way, spittin'
sand. "But if this old rattler don't show more speed,
Tremper and his posse is liable to catch up with us ag'in."
His mournful face is thoughtful as he starts suckin' on
one of his gold teeth, which is a little mannerism he's got
when he's schemin' somethin'. Soon he dispossesses himself. He says:

"This car is evident built fer coal, not sand. Sand bein'
heavier than coal, that's why they've only filled this car
a third up. In case of a bombardment from Tremper's
forces, we got cover to perfect ourselves and critters—"

"It's jist like a movin' fort, ain't it?" Blazin' Daylights
interrupts in boyish delight, poundin' sand out of his ear
at the same time.

"Yeah—but if it comes to a battle, we got to shoot over
their heads and not injure any of 'em or even kill 'em,
because we're jist a bunch of ramblin' rannies which ain't
got no friends in this Blue Butte country, and the posse
is composed of respectable cattlemen which would hang
us high like a tree if we made 'em too mad."

Blazin' Daylight's glad face changes to almost as mournful as what Schemer's is regular. "It's jist too bad. I feel
plumb like shootin' somebody. Well, I reckon we might as

well git on our hosses. I'll feel more natural in the saddle.
We can jist set and wait fer somethin' to happen."

We wasn't long settin' before it happened.

"Hey, down there," a hard-cooked voice hollers from
on top of the box car. "What is it, a circus? Where's your
tickets?"

"That's the conductor, and he's goin' to try and put us
off," cries Blazin' Daylights, his hand swoopin' fer his six-
gun.

"Easy, you sand-brained sap," Schemer remarks in an
undertone. "Didn't I jist explain we got to go easy on the
trigger?"

Blazin' Daylights represses himself, and the gorilla on
the box car climbs down aggressive on the grab-irons and
jumps into the sand car. He's a husky gazebo with a mean
face, and he's wearin' the regulation trainmen's high-bib
overalls and a blue shirt with white dots in it. Tucked
inside his bull neck he's got a red bandanna handkerchief.

He slogs up to Schemer, him bein' the closest.

"What are you ridin' on?" he snarls.

"Gladys," says Schemer, his long sad face not showin'
no emotion.

"Huh?"

"I mean my hoss."

"Yeah, I see you're on a hoss," the hombre says, kind
of out of the corner of his mouth. His hand is pullin'
nervous at the rawhide watch chain that trainmen always
keeps fastened to the special buttonhole in their overall
bib. "You look purty dizzy, too, sittin' on a hoss in a sand
car of a movin' train. But what I got reference to is: what
are you ridin' on, a ticket, or your funny looks? If you
ain't got a ticket, you got to git off, see?"

"Who the hell says so?" chips in Blazin' Daylights in
his deferential manner.

– 89 –

The gazebo's hand slips from his rawhide watch chain on past the special pocket where trainmen keeps their little notebooks and tin pencils, and on down toward his side. His jaw thrusts out ugly.

"I do, cowboy!"

"And you are whom, please, huh?" wants to know Schemer, polite.

"I'm the conductor, that's who I am. G'wan, git offa my train, all of you!" His eyes is glintin' mean now, and his hand starts slidin' a little behind him like he had a gun hid somewheres there.

"How are we gonna git our hosses off with the train movin'?" Schemer asks.

"You don't hafta git your hosses off. The railroad's got a right to hold 'em till you pay fer how far you've rode. I'll take care of your hosses, but you three boes gotta git off, and right now. G'wan, hit the cinders!"

The fella has got a bulldog scowl on his ugly pan, and he starts to step past Gladys's rear to git up closer to Schemer.

Schemer acts. More properly, he influences Gladys to act. It's near-human, the way they coöperates, them two, Schemer and Gladys. That little white-haired bronc kicks back, with the immediate and net result that this here loud-mouthed intruder, he gits himself bonged back agin' the side of the car.

Before he can draw that gun which his hand has been itchin' fer, we are all over him, and have took it away.

His note book and pencil falls out of his pocket durin' the mêlêe, and Schemer picks 'em up and replaces 'em. Likewise, Schemer sticks back that watch on its rawhide chain, which has fell out of his pocket. Then we tells this fella to git back to his caboose and stay there, because we'll throw *him* off if he comes back ag'in.

"That conductor is shore a mean-lookin' toad," Blazin'
Daylights contributes. "Why, it looks like he wanted to
steal our hosses, didn't it?"

Schemer don't say nothin', he bein' jist then polishin'
his gold teeth with a little sand which is still stuck on the
end of his tongue.

That fella which we've jist got through takin' a gun
from, he don't say nothin' either. Not till he's climbed
safe up on top the box car, he don't. Then he cusses us
out plenty, like all hell.

"There ain't nobody gonna make his bronc kick me
and take away my gun and git away with it," he clamors,
so frothin'-at-the-mouth mad that it makes us right nervous. "I'm comin' back agin' and shoot up everybody in
the car!"

"Now," says Blazin' Daylights to Schemer, "look what
you done, you and your 20-mule-team brains. Now the
conductor will come back with some brakemen and mebbe
a couple bulls and the fireman and engineer, and where
will we be? The answer is, we will be in the ditch. I might
as well of took a shot at him in the first place."

Schemer starts girdin' himself fer a defense of his actions, but he sees somethin' which makes him ferget all
about verbal arguments. He sees plain that it is a lead
argument which is goin' to be prevailin'.

Blazin' Daylights sees it too. "Tremper's posse!" he
blares.

Toppin' a grassy swell, and anglin' in toward the railroad, a dozen riders are ridin' like hell. When they sight
us in the sand car, they whoops and hollers and redoubles
their hosses' efforts, and some of 'em takes long potshots
at us with their guns.

"Reckon there ain't hardly no doubt about it," admits
the conservative Schemer. "They've crossed over the ridge

somewheres, and now they've pert near caught up with this old drag freight."

We don't no more'n git our hosses to lay down than, *whang*—the first bullet flattens out agin' the side of the gondola. *Ping*—another slug of lead does similar. They make a peculiar ringin' sound agin' the steel. And they're jist a starter. In another minute the air is so full of *whangs* and *pings*, it sounds like a Chinese orchestra.

Blazin' Daylights is positive entranced. As he starts slantin' over the side of the sand car to do a little blastin' with his own six-gun, Schemer grabs him by the shoulder.

"Don't fergit," he warns, "we got to shoot jist close enough to keep 'em from gittin' too close to the car, where they could mebbe push some of their lead bumble bees through our armor plate. We ain't shootin' to hit, remember!"

"I heard you the first twenty times," rejoins Blazin' Daylights, as he starts to seein' how close he can groove his bullets without actually scrapin' anybody. Schemer and me contributes our full quota of gunlead too, and altogether they is quite a metallic shower.

Then all of a sudden, Schemer notices somethin'. He divests himself of a yell, and we turn. Schemer indicates to the top of the swayin' box car, where a man in blue overalls and a red bandana handkerchief is squatted down and aimin' a revolver.

"The conductor!" Blazin' Daylights ejaculates. "Why, the old coyote-eatin' buzzard! He's gone and got himself another gun, he has, and he was gonna shoot us in the backs!"

"He *is* shootin'!" yells I.

"He *has* shot," corrects Schemer, as a bullet tears through his shirt right on a level with his heart.

Blazin' Daylights yanks up his gun, meanin' to shoot the revolver out of that would-be assassin's hand before another shot can be fired at Schemer. But Blazin' Daylights is a mile and a rod too slow. He never does git that shot in at all.

And why? Because Schemer, he has beat him to it. He has leveled up so quick that jist the friction of that gun movin' through the air is practically what sets the bullet off. Jist once he shoots, and that would-be assassin of his, he kind of hunches over, then topples off the box car to the cinders in plain sight of the posse, shot through the heart—dead.

Blazin' Daylights stares tongue-bound, while his mouth hangs open like a barn door. He is starin' at Schemer like he can't believe it; which is no wonder, because this is the first man Schemer has ever stopped cold with a bullet through the heart.

"You killed him," Blazin' Daylights finally gulps. "You killed the conductor!" He kind of shakes himself and demands fiercely: "What'd you do it fer, Schemer? And after all you been tellin' us not to shoot nobody! Right in front of the posse, that's mad at us anyway, you got to go kill yourself a conductor! Wouldn't of been no worse to kill a cowboy. You might as well of shot Ed Tremper himself. Now we are in one hell of a fix."

"Well, it was me or him," Schemer starts defendin' hisself, "and I like me better——"

"Yeah? Well, you see what we're in fer, don't you?" Blazin' Daylights demands, tragic. "We'll be all hunted criminals from justice fer the rest of our lives. We can't never have us no ranch of our own now and be cattle kings, but jist fugitives."

Blazin' Daylights was optimistic. "We don't even git a chance to be fugitives."

"Up your hands!" comes a hard voice from on top of the box car.

We whirls, but it is no use. Three separate and distinct

punchers has succeeded in swingin' off their hosses onto the freight train grab-irons a few cars back, and they have snuck forward over the decks, and now they're all three coverin' us.

We dump our artillery and put our hands up. That's all we can do.

One of the men climbs down between the cars and kicks the air, so that the freight train grinds to a quick stop.

Standin' there in the hands-up position, Blazin' Daylight's throat pulses a little, like as if he felt a rope was tied there. My own throat is got a constricted feelin' too. The only ray of possible sunshine is that Schemer is suckin' strenuous on one of his gold teeth.

The first ripe fruits of Schemer's molar massage is that he divests himself in this wise:

"Podners," he says to us, "I don't see Ed Tremper nowheres, do you? You could sight that old range pirate with his red face and black stubble beard on his big black hoss from a mile off. And he ain't here. Neither is any of these men his cowpunchers. I never seen any of 'em around Blue Butte, did you? The answer is 'No,' and the conclusion is that this ain't Ed Tremper's posse at all, but another and different and distinct posse, by hoss-fly!"

"You're right!" I says. "They have been shootin' us up by mistake. It's somebody else they're after, not us."

"K-rect."

"Then," says Blazin' Daylights, tryin' to make a raft out of a bale of watersoaked hay, "as soon as we tell 'em we're the wrong ones, we'll be all right."

"Well," says Schemer, a peculiar light in his mild eyes, "remember, I killed the conductor."

"Yeah," says a big sodbuster, climbin' over the side of the sand car like a old-time pirate boardin' on the Spanish Main, "you killed the conductor. And that ain't the biggest half of it, jasper. The bank cashier which you fellas shot up at Smoky Gulch, he died likewise."

"Haw-haw," laughs Blazin' Daylights, loud but not jubilant. "This is a joke on you! Somebody has robbed a bank, huh? And killed the cashier? And you been huntin' fer the outlaws, and you thought we was them? Haw-haw— this is a joke on you, because you got the wrong fellas. We ain't no outlaws, but respectable Bar X cowpokes from way down around Floatin' Rock Springs. Haw-haw," he finishes, some lame, though.

"Yeah," says that big sodbuster, who seems to be the leader, "it's a good joke. Haw-haw, we'll all laugh, haw-haw. And where did you say you put the bank's money?"

"Here's where the money is, boss," hollers one of the raidin' rannies, who has been investigatin' in Schemer's saddle bag.

"That's all I wanta know," the leader says, hard-boiled. "Put a hobble on these three nice boys, and we'll go enjoy ourselves a hangin'."

Well, it shore looks like the last ace has been played fer us box-car buckaroos. And jist such a short time before the future was stretchin' brightly away into the smilin' sun with a promise of us bein' cattle kings and sittin' in our cool ranch house smokin' big ceegars.

At this desperate juncture, Schemer unleashes himself with this: "As a dyin' request, gents, will you take a look at that ape I shot off the top of the box car?"

"You mean that poor innocent conductor which you killed in cold-blood?"

"It's a argumentative point, seein' as I shot in immediate defense of my life and after he drawed first—and he wasn't the conductor of the train, anyway."

Blazin' Daylights and me perks up and stares with speechless hope.

"Huh?" says the posse leader. "Who was he if he wasn't the conductor?"

"He was one of the fellas which robbed your bank. He seemed a little bulky around the waist, didn't you think? Mebbe he's wearin' a money belt with the bank's money in it—I dunno. You better see. While you're about it, why don't you detail a couple of your warriers to round up them two fellas——" He motions onexcited at two men which have broken from the standin' train and are running away fast over the countryside. "I dunno, but they might be confederates of the alleged conductor."

Well, by hoss-fly, Schemer was right! Right about every one of them things. The three men, the dead one and the two escapin' live ones, was all caught, and they had the bank's money on 'em. They was positive identified as the outlaws which the posse was huntin' fer!

The real train crew comes up from the caboose when they're sure the shootin' is over, and they are some surprised to see the three bandits which had been ridin' their rattler and masqueradin' as trainmen to further their escape.

"I betcha," says Blazin' Daylights to Schemer, "that you knowed all the time when you shot him that he was a desperate criminal and not a conductor."

"I had a notion," admits Schemer, modest.

"How in hell did you know?" the now admirin' herd of waddies and trainmen clamors to find out.

"Well," Schemer obliges, "I got a habit of noticin' little things. And they was shore a lot of little things wrong. I have met enough trainmen while nursemaidin' steers to Omaha and Chicago to know what trainmen mostly wears and looks like. In the first place"—he points around to the crew—"you don't see none of these boys wearin' red bandannas on their necks, do you? The answer is 'No,' they are wearin' blue ones. But this here bank robber and cashier killer, he had on a red one. That wasn't none conclusive, but it steamed up my suspicions.

"They was still more steamed when I seen what a mean look he had on his face, more like a desperado than a conductor. And he was so uncommon anxious to git hold of our hosses. Furthermore, conductors mostly don't pack revolvers, especially six-guns. Bulls, mebbe; not conductors. Even more further, when I picked up the pencil and note book after the fight, I noticed the pencil didn't have no lead in it, or the note book no writin'. Nary a single car number or nothin' in it.

"Furthermore even than that, his watch is a dollar watch, and who ever heard of a conductor runnin' a train on a dollar watch? The watch wasn't runnin' anyway, and I smelled likker on his breath. In consequence of all of which I deduced he wasn't the conductor."

The posse leader is all fer takin' Schemer back to the county seat and gittin' him appointed official deputy in charge of detectin' crime, but Schemer refuses the offer kindly, sayin' he has got cattle problems at home requirin' immediate attention.

As the train starts up, with us settin' our hosses ag'in in the sand car, and the cheers of the admirin' posse grows dim, Blazin' Daylights turns to Schemer and says, kind of irate:

"I'm as plumb anxious as what you are to git back to the old Bar X and buy in on that little ranch at Floatin' Rock Springs. And special now that we will have some reward money comin' fer the capture of the desperadoes, to add to our original six thousands of dollars. We can buy more cows to start and become cattle kings quicker. All the same, I'm sore about you refusin' the boys' kind invite to go back to that bank-robbery town and let 'em throw a big drink and dance to-night for our honor. We could 'a' had anything we wanted from the boys, as they was in a meller mood; but all the boon you went and craved is fer the engineer to show some speed with this old rattler. I got me a notion to hop right off!"

"Mebbe," says Schemer, "you never noticed what I noticed, kickin' dust way back there in between them two hills, see?" He points. "That big black hoss in the lead— think hard if you ever seen him before."

Blazin' Daylights squints agin' the sun. "Tremper!" he explodes. "Tremper and his posse, still on our trail!"

"K-rect."

But the fireman is a-firin' coal, and the engineer is a-settin' on the throttle. The cars sway and the wheels click faster and faster over the rail joints, and Tremper's posse gits dimmer and dimmer, till it is swallowed up by dusty distance.

Us box-car buckaroos, we all leans out of the saddle and shakes each other's hands.

Sea Fever

IN 1848, BEFORE the first nugget was picked up below Sutter's mill on the American River, not more than a half dozen ships dropped anchor along the whole coast of California. The next year seven hundred vessels dumped one hundred thousand roaring 49ers on the new wharfs at San Francisco.

One of these new arrivals was young Maine-coast sailor-man, Seth Harper. Seth was about the only one who had *not* come to California to dig gold.

Seth was a salt-water sailor, pure and simple. Since he had been old enough to haunt the wharves at Portland, and monkeyshine his way along a ship's rigging, he had known that a life at sea was the only thing for him.

A slim and shaggy 17, but looking older, Seth's particular inspiration was a young man named Jacob Webb who, at the age of 24, captained that famous Baltimore clipper, *Neptune*. Seth had always been quietly certain that before he was 24, he, too, would have his own ship.

But that was before he came under the baleful stare and the hard hand of Captain Comstock. Now, as Seth went ashore at the boiling new port of San Francisco with his seabag on his shoulder, he wasn't even sure he wanted to remain a sailor on *any* ship. He thought he might just as well head out with the rest of these madmen for the goldfields.

Seth had sailed coastwise from Portland on short runs in New England and Canadian tidewater, but this trip around Cape Horn was his first deep-water voyage. And on this first trip it had been his dire misfortune to draw a berth with the yankee clipper *Half Moon*, captained by that red-faced, bull-necked roarer, Gilford Comstock, also from down in Maine.

Whether it was ginseng and furs to China, or tea and silk *from* China, whoever got there first with the cargo sold at the top market prices. So the ship owners called for speed and more speed—and speed was what Captain Comstock gave them.

To get this kind of speed, New England ship builders had to design a new kind of ship. They built one they called a clipper—a ship with long, sharp lines, and square-rigged sails reaching to the skies. The sail area of some clippers could be measured by the acre.

Clipper ships had cut half the time from the old sailing schedules, and had nearly driven the duck-shaped, fore-and-aft rigged vessels off the tradeways. The new brand of ship called for a new breed of sailor. And it called for a captain who knew how to drive a ship—and men—for all they were worth, and who dared to do so.

Captain Comstock was such a driver. He had been one of the first to get sea legs under him in the China trade, in which he had persistently broken sailing-time records, even his own. He did the same thing on the Liverpool-Australia run. And on this present run from Boston to San Francisco he had beat around the Horn in winter gales to bring the *Half Moon* through the Golden Gate in less than one hundred days, and only two days short of an all-time record.

To do this he had crowded on sail, and driven his crew incessantly in all kinds of weather. The last to take in sail upon the approach of a gale wind, Captain Comstock was the first to put it out again when a storm abated. Sometimes he didn't reef at all, but drove his clipper full-rip with the wind, the tall masts bending like a hunter's bow, at the risk of breaking to crash amidship and drag their dangling weight overside, grieviously imperiling the ship and everyone on it.

Ship owners esteemed him because he kept their cargos moving, thereby putting more and more money in their tills. Men who sailed before the mast looked at the captain differently. In sailors' boardinghouses and ships' fo'c'sles he was known as the "demon of the seas." His name brought scowls, threats, and curses. So young Seth Harper couldn't say he hadn't been warned. He had sailed with Captain Comstock anyway, reasoning that he had things to learn from this salt-crusted old seadog, and being youthfully confident that however arduous the slave-driving, he could take it.

Well, he *had* taken it. That wasn't to say he liked it, or had to take it again.

But now at the head of the wharf he had to pass Captain Comstock. A truculent bull of a man, the Captain stood spread-legged, wearing a dirty visored cap, and chewing a dry West Indies cheroot. He might have stepped aside to let Seth pass. But he didn't. He stayed there, a wicked glint in his eyes, and his flint-knuckled fists hanging loose at his sides from under the short sleeves of his worn sea jacket.

Seth stopped in front of him, sourly mindful that he wasn't on the ship now; he didn't have to take this old slave-driver's guff. At the same time he remembered something that had happened off the Argentine coast when they were heading into a *pampero*, the gale that blows out of the hundred-mile mouth of the La Plata River with raw foretaste of what would be everyday fare if a vessel lived to round Cape Horn.

On that day the mate's order had gone out to close-reef the skysails. A sailor had taken a scared look at the bending mast a hundred and seventy feet high, and the tight canvas up there, glazed to boiler-plate stiffness by a coating of ice. The long yardarms would be ice-coated too, and he would have to work his way out on one while it was pitching and swaying. Then, with sleet in his face, and the wind clawing, he would have to fist the frozen sails, beat the canvas limp before he could take it in.

The sailor moved to the unwelcome task, but slowly.

"Come alive," the mate bawled. "Out of the graveyard!"

The sailor didn't move any faster.

That was when Captain Comstock moved in. The sailor was fully as big as the captain, but the captain squashed him to the deck with one swung fist. The sailor had to be carried to his bunk . . . and the captain had turned his bleak-eyed stare on Seth.

Seth took pride in being a "topman" sailor. The wildest swinging yardarms held no terrors for him. In daylight or darkness, in any kind of weather, he could climb anywhere and do the job that needed to be done. Under the captain's barked orders, he did this one. But he seethed at the brutal way the captain had handled his shipmate; and as brutalities crowded one on another in the grueling days that followed, his sympathies had come to rest wholly with the rebellious crew. To the last man they were sullenly determined to jump ship as soon as it reached San Francisco. *If* it ever reached San Francisco.

Rounding the Horn, there were times when it appeared certain that the captain's hard driving was going to put the clipper under a thousand fathoms of icy water. The Cape wind never stopped, and every keening gust of it seemed to be blowing straight off the South Pole. They were eighteen days beating around the tip of del Fuego before they even approached the worst of it, the Diego Ramirez Reefs where rip tides of the Atlantic and Pacific met in unpredictable walls of churning water.

Everything that could blow away had been tied down or taken below, and lifelines had been put out for the meager protection they afforded when the seas swept across the decks in a solid, pounding weight of water. Every horrendous tale that Seth had ever heard about the Cape Horn passage came true. Under the blast of the storm winds the *Half Moon* shuddered and heaved. Old seadogs liked to tell about a ship rolling so far over you had to climb the walls. Seth climbed them. The clipper rolled so far over it was a mercy she ever came back, especially with her spars and rigging so heavy with ice that her own topweight was enough to sink her. It was nearly impossible to keep a fire going below. Icy water dripped through the deck, and the ship took water through her seams. The pumps were kept going twenty-four hours a day.

Another ship's master might have turned back to wait for fairer weather, but not Captain Comstock. He would bull it through if it took every man and every sail off his ship. Sometimes it seemed as though nothing but his savage will was holding the creaking, wallowing clipper together.

And then came the day when a yardarm broke and crashed to the deck from the high mizzenmast. The plunging wooden spar brought the reefed sail and a few tons of ice down with it.

A sailor, little Abbie Spring from Newburyport, was caught under the falling weight and pinned cruelly to the deck. They heard the scream that was pinched off in his throat, and they thought that surely he had been killed outright. But his whimperings continued above the ship's creakings and the sea's roaring. A miracle Little Abbie under that jumble of wreckage was still alive.

Seth Harper was closest. He had been chopping footholds in the ice-caked deck. As quickly as he could on that heaving, slippery surface he put his axe to the wreckage, trying to chop Abbie clear.

From behind Seth the captain's voice sounded in an angry bellow. "Leave him be, boy. Jump lively. Chop that spar away."

Held by one of the mizzenmast stays, the broken spar dangled its ponderous weight over the side, heeling the ship over. Seth reasoned that a man's life was more important than anything else at this moment. Disregarding the captain's order, he kept working in a frenzy to free Little Abbie of that part of the wreckage which pinned him down.

"Boy, do you hear me?" the captain's voice roared again. "Get to that hanging spar! Chop it away!"

Seth gave no heed to the captain's order, but continued chopping with all the life that was in him, to save the life of Little Abbie.

The next he knew was when he felt the captain's hand drop like a club on his shoulder. The hand yanked him violently backwards to the tilting deck. Seth let go the axe and scrambled to keep from sliding overboard into that maelstrom of churning ice and water that beat at the ship's side.

The captain put out no hand to save him, but instead grabbed up the axe and in a fury put his arms and shoulders to the task of cutting the stay that held the wreckage dangling overside. Not until he had cut it away did he turn to that part of the wreckage which held Little Abbie pinned. He released Little Abbie and motioned two sailors to pick up the broken body and carry it below.

Then he turned his bleak stare on Seth. "You disobeyed my orders, boy. That's mutiny. Sailors have rotted out a voyage in irons for less. Get below."

Seth was spared the bread and water diet and the iron shackles only because all hands were needed to work the ship. Especially now that Little Abbie was gone; he lived through the night, but died early the next morning. The captain got it back at Seth in another way. He saw that the mates consistently gave him the most disagreeable and arduous jobs—or so it seemed to Seth.

Seth stood up to it. They hadn't broken him. And the nightmare was all behind him now. They had reached San Francisco. He was off the ship. He was on the wharf with his seabag on his shoulder, a free man, beholden to nobody.

There was only this little matter of Captain Comstock barring his way, standing in front of him, refusing to budge and let him past. There was a black look in the captain's eyes. A look hard to read. Seth thought at first it mirrored only contempt. But if he hadn't known the captain so well he might then have judged the expression held a hint of human loneliness.

The captain spoke first. "Off for the goldfields, boy?"

"If I feel like it," young Harper told him. He was off the ship now, out from under the captain's authority, and he didn't add, "Sir."

"You're a good sailor." The words came grudgingly from the captain's gross lips. "You've got salt in your veins. You'll be back."

"Not to your ship, I won't."

With the words Seth felt tension drain away. It was

something he had wanted to say for a long time. But he had seen men beaten to the deck for saying less. The captain would rightly take the refusal to serve on his ship as a calculated insult. Well, let him.

Seth braced himself for whatever might come. He shifted his seabag. He could heave it in the captain's face. After that he might go down, but he'd give a good account of himself first.

But the captain only shrugged and said gruffly, "That's for you to decide. Off my ship a man doesn't need the captain to tell him what to do."

Captain Comstock stepped aside.

Seth exchanged an uncertain look with him. Deep in the hard coldness of those sea-gray eyes there seemed to be a flickering of human warmth. It was almost as though he wanted to say something in his defense. But he didn't say anything. Nothing at all.

Seth decided he was imagining the whole business. He shifted his seabag and strode past the captain, walking with resolution and not looking back.

Off the wharf Seth was swallowed up in the ferment of boomtown activity. San Francisco was still a stick-and-canvas town, though building fast. Saloons and gambling houses were the main stay, but outfitters for the gold fields were opening up. Warehouses, boarding houses, and restaurants.

Seth saw incredible signs: *One Egg One Dollar* . . . *Hand-Sewn Boots—$100*. It wasn't a golden egg and it was an ordinary looking pair of boots. Pitchmen kept up a line of fast talk in front of dives and barrel-houses. And around the clock the poker and faro dealers sat in their wide-bottomed chairs and kept the card games going.

After three months of lonely sky and water, Seth was

both excited and repelled as he made his patient way through the mud of the crooked streets in company with horses, drays, flies, and jostling men. At nearly every step he shrugged off grifters and bunko-artists who judged a sailor fresh from a ship to be easy pickings. A man even tried to sell him a grubby handful of "genuine gold nuggets fresh from the diggings—cheap."

"Seth! Hey you—Seth. Come on in here, lad."

Seth brightened at sound of the familiar voice. He looked up to see one of his shipmates motioning him from inside the wide opened door of a place that said SILVER PALACE on a big fancy sign outside.

Seth went in. Inside, the place looked more like a stockyards pen than a silver palace. Sawdust on a dirt floor, and pine planks put across the tops of some barrels for a bar. But his shipmate pounded his back and said with excitement firing his eyes, "You never saw anything like it. Miners comin' in from the diggings . . . pouring gold dust across the bar from their leather pokes like it was common as yellow cornmeal."

Seth hadn't yet got into the spirit of things. "What's the use of going after it if that's all you're going to do with it afterwards?"

"Hey, you're too serious," his shipmate said. "Loosen up, lad. These miners are living high. Havin' a roaring bang-up time. When their gold's gone, they'll go and get more. I'm goin' too. Everybody is."

Uphill and downhill in the raw new town of Frisco, everywhere that Seth wandered that day, it was the same: gold-fevered talk. A town full of wild men, with only the gamblers and bartenders remaining calm; and most of the gold, it seemed to Seth, going steadily to them.

On his second day in Frisco he saw a man shot down. Seth didn't know what the provocation might have been, but he did see the man bleeding away his life in the sawdust on the saloon floor—with the man who shot him walking away, unhurried, to disappear in the throng outside.

There was no law in this city. None worthy of the name. No one cared, or even seemed to notice much what went on. There was nobody to tell anybody what to do, so each man did whatever he wanted, or whatever anybody else would let him do. If somebody got hurt in the process, that was just his bad luck.

Seth felt a sudden need to get out somewhere under the sun and breathe some fresh air. A bent little white-haired man wearing a dusty sombrero followed him out.

"I been watching you in there, sonny," the little old man said frankly. "You didn't appear to like what you was looking at."

"Did you?" Seth asked.

"No more'n you, sonny. That's why I'm talking to you. How about it; you tied up on any kind of speculation?"

"I'm my own man, if that's what you mean."

"That's *jist* what I mean." From under the rim of the old sombrero blue eyes probed Seth keenly. "You appear to be a clean-cut lad, and I'm a man who acts on his first impressions. What would you say to a partnership in a gold mine?"

In spite of the bluntness of the proposition—or maybe because of it—Seth had the impression that this was the first honest proposition he had listened to in this gold-crazy town.

"You've got a claim?" he asked.

"A good one, sonny. But I need young hands to help me work it. Honest hands. I been in town two weeks now, just lookin' and lookin'."

"How do you know there's gold there?"

"Got to be. I spent my whole life lookin'. I know."

"You ever find other places that looked this good?"

The old man's eyes went far away and dreamy. "Plenty. I found plenty of places. They never paid off quite. This'n will."

Seth smiled. "You never get discouraged, do you, old timer?"

"No sir-ee. I keep scroungin'. This riff-raff you see in this town—" He spread his arms wide in disdain. "All they want to do is get the gold and get out. If they don't find it first-off they quit. And if one of 'em does find some, likely he'll drop it right here. We won't do that, sonny. Workin' together, we'll hit it big and hold it tight."

Seth could feel it now—the shimmering lure of the gold fields that put a fever in the blood of every man in this restless town. A tingle ran through him to his fingertips. The last of his uncertainty and doubt died away. After he had separated himself from the old man, he walked with a new spring to his step.

"Remember where I'm dug in here," the old-timer called after him. "The Globe Hotel. You come in any time and we'll work ourselves out the details."

But it wasn't the Globe Hotel that drew Seth. It was the yankee clipper, *Half Moon*. He found Captain Comstock in the wheelhouse, and lowered his seabag to the floor.

"Changed my mind, sir," he said. "I'll be ready to go when the *Half Moon* sails, if there's still a berth for me."

Looking at him, the Captain showed no expression. "You get the gold fever out of your blood, boy?"

"Not quite, sir. But sea fever's worse, you might say."

The captain said nothing, and Seth went on, "I had one good sounding proposition. But when I thought on it, it was just a dream. Not even my dream. Another man's."

"And your dream's a deck under your feet heaving to salt water?"

Coming from Captain Comstock's gross mouth, the word "dream" sounded out of place. But Seth accepted it at face value and said, "You might put it that way, sir."

"Then," the captain said, "I take you to be either a brave man or a foolish one."

"How so, sir?"

"To sail twice with the demon of the sea?"

Seth smiled. Incredibly, the captain smiled too, then sobered and said stiffly, "Any man who's lived aboard a ship as long as I have—I find it hard to say the important things. A captain's lot is a lonesome one. That time you saw me beat the man to the deck for dragging his heels at the mate's order—the man was a chronic malingerer. His attitude at the moment was endangering the safety of the ship."

"I realize that now, sir, since I've had time to think it over."

The captain said, stiffly still, "I don't want to appear to be justifying myself—or maybe I do. That time off the Cape was an even more pointed case. It was a case of first things first. The danger was immediate to the whole crew, Little Abbie included. In that running sea, with that spar hanging over the side, canting the ship, every second was important—"

"I understand, sir."

"You agree, then, to my way of handling things aboard ship?" A curious question for a ship's master to ask a crewman; and more curious still, something about the captain's manner made Seth feel that importance was attached to the answer.

Seth said, "Since you ask me, sir, I seriously question the need for so much harshness. But I don't question the need for authority on a ship. When the safety of all can be imperiled by one, *somebody has to be recognized by everybody* as being in command. Somebody has to tell people what to do. Even on land I've been noticing they could use a little of this, sir."

The captain stared hard at him. "You know that the trip back will be a nightmare compared to the one here. I've already lost most of my crew to the gold camps. What I'll get will be water-front scum . . . and if I'm lucky a few landlubber Chinese or Mexicans. They'll all have to be whipped into sea-shape. I'll earn my name for sure on the way back."

"I understand that, sir."

"Then you're hired."

"Thank you, sir." Seth turned and started with his seabag to the sailors' fo'c'sle.

"You're going the wrong way, Mr. Harper," the captain called after him.

Seth stopped, a slow tingle running through him to his finger ends, precisely as it had on shore. On board a ship the word "Mister" was reserved for officers.

"Stow your gear in Mr. Bell's room," the captain said. "He's gone to the gold fields too. I have to have someone to help me drive this ship. You're the *Half Moon's* new second mate, Mr. Harper."

The Eskimo Express

"Slim" Collins was down on his luck. He hadn't had a break for so long that he wouldn't know one if it came to him diamond-hitched and labeled. Ever since he had come over the border it had been this way. This Far North country was the bunk—no place for a workingman; he'd tell that to the cockeyed world.

As he stumped slowly along the main drag of that little Canadian fur post of Caribou Bend, there was a bulldog set to Slim's firm young jaw. His rundown boot heels creaked on the dry snow, and his breath trailed behind him in the thirty-below cold like steam from a lumber-camp locomotive.

His frost-rimmed eyes, closed to slits against the glare of the morning sun, looked out from behind the upturned collar of a ragged mackinaw. There was a glint of desperation in those humorous, blue eyes.

Down on his luck was right! The cold wasn't the worst of it. He was hungry. Two full days now since he had clamped teeth on anything more nourishing than the ends of his moosehide mitts. He was a stranger in Caribou Bend. It wasn't his nature to ask for food, and he couldn't find any kind of work.

The nervous *yarp-yarp* of a team of dogs drawn up across the street caught his attention. Big, rangy brutes, dirty gray in color, the dogs looked like wolves to Slim. The light *komatik* to which they were hitched stood directly in front of the Canadian Exploration Company's office.

That must be the very team he had *almost* been hired to take out last night. He grimaced. What a high-powered dumb bat he was, to have admitted that he had never driven a dog team. Fellow across there had wanted a driver the worst way.

He paused, attracted by loud talk from within the doorway across the street. One man was tongue-lashing another. He was speaking in a high-pitched, nasal voice.

"Why, you yellow, sniveling punk!" he railed. "You haven't got the guts of a two-week-old white fox! Didn't I fix everything nice for you? Didn't I? What? Didn't I furnish a brand-new Colt automatic? And now when we're all set, you quit me cold!"

Slim's ears perked up. That little dough ball with the red, moon face and the disagreeable voice was the same man who had been looking for some one to drive a dog team.

"But I didn't know about those hold-ups," Slim heard the other man grumble sullenly. "I didn't know about Black Bruele when I told you I'd do it."

The fat man squawked excitedly:

"Who's Black Bruele? A thieving bush-sneak breed, that's all. And you—you let a man like that scare you—"

"Aw, go stick your head in the snow!" The other started disgustedly away. "Take out some life insurance on that fat paunch of yours," he flung back, "and do the job yourself!"

Trembling with anger, the little fat man entered his office. Slim hurried over.

"I'll take that job, mister," he said, bursting in at the door.

"What job?"

"Any job! The job that guy just quit." Slim worked his

head out from behind the frayed mackinaw collar. He was grinning. "I don't care what it is—I can do it."

The man took one look at the week's growth of stubble on Slim's face. Then his eyes dropped to the patched and threadbare clothes.

His plump hand went up in a little, jerking wave.

"Outside, bum," he growled.

The friendly grin left Slim's face. His chisel chin thrust out belligerently, and his fists clenched within his mitts. The man backed away, a startled look on his moon face. Slim took a threatening step toward him. The man's eyes went wide with fear.

Slim laughed harshly.

"No, I'm not gonna clip you, Doughball. They lock a guy up for that in this country. You're safe in your office, all right. But you better take six men with you, see, next time you step outside."

Slim stormed out. In front of the door he paused a moment, taking stock. He was too free with his fists, that's what he was. He'd come near letting "Doughball" have it in there. He had to be more careful. His front wasn't so hot now, and he was too far from home and friends to take chances. Canadian law worked on a hair-trigger. Better be free, with an empty stomach, than eat in jail.

He had to eat something some time, though. Hungry? Just to look at that sleek team of Huskies in the street there made his mouth water. He could wrap his tongue around any two of those dogs and swallow them raw and wiggling. Yes, and top-off on the harness!

His glance traveled on back from the team to the speed-*komatik*. His eyes brightened. That passenger sled looked to be all set for a long trip. Wouldn't they be taking food on a long trip? Man, they would!

He looked quickly up and down the street. No one in

sight. He flashed a glance through the door behind him. Doughball didn't seem to be noticing. With an elaborate air of carelessness, he sidled up to the sled.

Once there, he acted quickly. Reaching under the bearskin robe, he pawed around in search of anything that looked like food. His hand didn't connect. He burrowed deeper into the coverings, bending far over the sled. He wouldn't take much—just enough to melt the edge off his hunger. He had to live, damn it—

There was a high-pitched shriek behind him, then the loud roar of a gun. A bullet creased so close that he could have counted the rifling marks.

The dogs *ki-yied* and flung their weight against the harness. The light sled lurched; Slim lost his balance and sprawled awkwardly across it. Two more shots split the air above him. The dogs clawed in frenziedly, and tore down the street.

With his long legs dangling, Slim held on like grim death to the framework of that wildly gyrating *komatik*. The outfit was gathering speed. More shots came from behind, but the crazily swooping sled made a difficult target.

As soon as he could, Slim worked around into a more secure position and looked back from his flying perch. Yes, it was Doughball, all right, causing all this ruction. Where did he get off trying to kill a fellow just for trying to swipe a loaf of bread or something?

The old hunk of lard wasn't shooting any more now; he was waddling down the street like a scared walrus looking for a water hole.

Say, there was another dog outfit down there! Doughball must be going to get somebody to chase him! Well, let 'em come. They'd never catch this old Eskimo express.

The dogs skidded the *komatik* around a curve at the

outskirts of the Post. The crack of a whip and a confusion of shouts told Slim that somebody had started in pursuit.

Rummaging around in the bed of furs, Slim found a whip there. He cracked the rawhide clumsily over the backs of the dogs.

"Hi-ya—gid-dap—mush," he shouted.

He didn't know if it was the "hi-ya" or the "gid-dap" or the "mush" that worked. Anyway, the dogs strained against their breast straps in a burst of speed. Slim arranged the fur lap robe snugly about him.

He was grinning now. He thrilled to the icy rush of air against his face, and the whine of sled runners against the trail-hard snow. Hey, this was the nuts! And nothing to it! What did it matter if he didn't know a malemute from a toboggan? He cracked the long whip again.

"Gid-dap, dogs. Hi-ya— Hey, what the all-fired blazes—"

The whip had tangled in the dog harness, and the end of the rawhide, trailing back, had gone under the runners. The sled swayed drunkenly. Slim dropped the whip handle and held on with both hands. Too late! The sled hit a bump, careened crazily on one runner, and went over. The drifted snow into which the *komatik* overturned, piled up in front and jerked the dogs to a stop.

Slim worked frantically to dig out the snow-bogged outfit. From the corner of his eye he kept watch on that other sled which was bearing down upon him.

"Hi-ya, dogs! Mush! Gid-dap!" he shouted the second he had the sled righted on the trail.

A revolver shot from behind helped out his urgings. The Huskies leaped ahead. Slim ran along a few steps, then threw himself belly bumper on the fast-moving sled.

There were more revolver shots, but the man pursuing was not yet within accurate range. The staccato pistol

shots merely served to excite Slim's team and spur it on.
With a grim satisfaction glinting in his eyes, Slim saw his
rangy dogs pull rapidly away from those others. Boy, some
team he had here. Pulling fools!

Sitting up, he scooped the snow out of the *komatik* and
fixed the furs snugly about him again. He added his own
lusty voice to the excited barkings of the dogs. But he did
not touch the whip.

These animals were a picked team, it seemed. Sled-
broke and swift. There was a well-defined trail. O.K.,
he'd let the dogs have their heads. After a while he'd have
to decide where he was going. But now—

Food! That's what he wanted—food. Raising his head
occasionally to yell out a "gid-dap" or a "mush," he continued the search he had started in Caribou Bend. First
he turned up a padlocked leather satchel. He shook it.
Papers. No food in there.

Ransacking further, he found a .45 Colt automatic and
a few extra clips, bullet-filled. A short-handled ax was
brought to light, also. And a big block of what appeared
to be fish.

The fish was for the dogs, of course. He looked further.
He practically tore the sled to pieces in his search. No
luck. The sled was as bare of things to eat as an Eskimo
igloo at the end of the Moon-of-the-Deep-Snows. Nothing
but food for dogs.

Slim turned dubious eyes toward that hunk of raw, frozen fish. Suddenly he grabbed up the ax. Hacking off a
small piece of the fish, he held it to his nose and sniffed.
Not much smell. Well—dogs ate it, and Indians, he'd
heard, ate dogs. Well— He bolted the fish and waited,
pop-eyed, for something to happen. Nothing did. He
hacked off a bigger piece.

A little later, heaving a sigh, he settled back and gazed

lazily at the white landscape scudding past. Hey, but this was traveling in style! Warm furs, a good old *komatik*, a crack dog team—and a stomach full of frozen fish. If the folks at home could see him now!

All at once, for no apparent reason, the merry, carefree look faded out of Slim's eyes. His shoulders sagged and his face grew as long and dour as an arctic night.

He was in the devil's own mess! Bucking the Mounted Police! In the excitement of the chase and all, he hadn't thought about it from this angle. Bet he'd be tagged for a criminal now all over the Dominion. On the dodge from redcoat law. And the Mounted always got their man.

Back in the States they used to hang a fellow for stealing a horse. Just a horse without any wagon. Here he'd stolen a speed-*komatik* which was certainly the equal of any old ranch cart. Yes, and a whole flock of dogs! Good dogs, too, thoroughbreds, judging from the way they had left that other team like it was running backward. How many dogs like these would it take to be the same as one horse? At the very least, he must have the equivalent of two horses and one wagon here. If they'd hang a man for stealing one mangy horse—

He groaned, in his imagination feeling that seven-times-around hemp knot against his ear.

Of course, the way he had taken this outfit—it had been a kind of special thing. But you couldn't always depend on the law to recognize special things.

Well, if he was a criminal now, the quicker he started thinking and acting like one, the better it would be for him. Let's see, now—the first thing would be to shake the evidence, get rid of these dogs. He had read a lot of Western stories about horse thieves. Almost always the thief was caught riding the horse.

He thought a moment. Gradually a look of panic crept into his eyes. Why—he *couldn't* shake this outfit!

He had no snowshoes. If he left the sled, he'd have to stay on the trail. On foot he'd be taken like a crippled rabbit being nabbed by an arctic fox.

No, he'd have to stay with this damning evidence, the evidence that, at the worst, could hang him, and at the very best could land him a long prison sentence.

About noon of the short Northern day, Slim suddenly came to a fork in the trail.

"Whoa, dogs! Hey, stop—whoa!"

The dogs loped on, noses down, bushy tails held high.

"Hey, whoa! Take a rest," Slim shouted desperately. "Don't you wanta rest? Whoa!"

How did you stop these brutes, anyway? There weren't any lines to pull on. No wheels to break.

Just before the lead dog reached the fork in the trail, Slim found a way. Throwing his weight heavily to one side, he upset the sled.

Clambering out of the drift, looking like an animated snow man, he stood pondering for a moment. He didn't know where either of these roads led. Probably best to take the least-traveled route. He was rated as a bandit now, and the less people a fugitive bandit had to meet, the better it was for the bandit. Sure.

This was high ground here. He could see in all directions. Might as well rest the dogs a minute, and feed 'em their fish.

Resting here, Slim kept a close watch on the back trail. It was well he did. Before the sharp commands of the driver reached his ears, before he heard the crack of the whip, he saw that pursuing sled swing into distant view.

Running up alongside the dogs, Slim shouted and waved his arms wildly, trying to *shoo* the animals toward the dim trail.

The dogs refused to be *shooed*. Some of them barked at him, some ruffed their shaggy throats and growled. One big, wolfish gray accorded him a superior stare, and laid down in the harness. Slim aroused him with the toe of his boot.

That seemed to decide the dogs. The whole team pulled, and Slim hopped on the sled as it swung past.

This trail was not so hard-packed. It was slower going now. But his pursuers would be slowed too. It would all even out in the long run. This trail, Slim thought, must lead to an isolated mining camp somewhere back in the hills. He could leave this outfit there for the owner to find. Sell this Colt automatic or something, and so get food and a pair of snowshoes. With the rackets, he could take to the open timber, make a try at working through to a railroad somewhere before they caught him. A long shot—yes—but his only chance.

The sky was a pale-greenish color, and bright with a leaden sheen. A blazing murky ball, the sun in the southwest hung low over a thin, gray line of forest. For several hours now the trail had wound through a region of rolling hills. The slopes grew steeper as Slim drove on, and he took to getting off the *komatik* and helping the dogs on the up grades. Here and there dense groves of jack pines relieved the barrenness of the white landscape.

It was late in the afternoon when tragedy settled upon Slim.

At a place where the snow-mantled trees crowded the dog train on both sides, Slim was startled by the near-by *cr-aa-ck* of a rifle. A bullet tore through his bearskin lap robe!

As though the first shot were a signal, other shattering *cr-aa-cks* sounded from the purple shadows of the pines on both sides of the trail. Caught between a murderous cross fire, Slim flung himself flat on the sled.

"Gid-dap," he howled at the dogs. "Gid-dap—mush—whoopee—kit!"

Something of his desperate need seemed to make itself felt to the dogs. Lunging against their harness, they pulled like devils. The sled flew.

But so were bullets flying. Lead was riddling the *komatik*, and whanging past to slug into the snow.

It was clear that the ambushers were taking little time to aim. They were relying more on a lucky bullet finding its mark. But with rifle lead spattering around like buckshot, how could he hope to pull clear without stopping some of it?

He winced involuntarily as a bullet fanned so close to his ear that he could feel the air wake.

Rummaging frenziedly under the lap robe in search of the Colt automatic, he kept his eyes on that short turn in the trail dead ahead. If he could reach the turn he would be safe. He hadn't been hit yet. Maybe he could make it. Maybe—

A bullet splintered through the sled beneath him. Another brought a yelp of pain from one of the dogs.

Flashing a look, he saw the nearest dog had gone lame. He was leaving a trail of blood in the snow with every footfall.

"Come on, boy," Slim pleaded.

Finally his groping hand closed over the automatic. The team was close to that turn in the trail now. Close. Rifles were still cracking, bullets picking snow from under the sled runners. But just around the turn was safety. The close-pressing pines would be a shield against this raining death. A new chance for life. Just around the turn.

A bullet snarled through the cloth of his mackinaw, and brought a sharp twinge of pain to his side. He gritted his teeth. Take more than a hot slug grazing his ribs to stop him.

There! The lead dog had made the turn. The second dog was around! Another. All of them! With snow spuming white from beneath the runners, the sled, too, skidded around.

No immediate danger now from behind. But Slim was looking ahead, and what he saw wrenched a cry of despair from his lips.

A man, hard-faced and resolute, crouched at the edge of the trail, coolly leveling a revolver. He was a big man, and he wore a black fur parka. Crouched there, he looked like some huge grizzly.

The man must have been planted here as a last resort, Slim realized, in case the ambushers missed. That gun barrel looked as big as a hollow log.

Self-possession did not leave Slim. Shifting his weight on the *komatik*, he overturned it in the snowdrift just as he had done before when he wanted to stop. At the same instant he exchanged shots with the man at the side of the road. Their bullets went wild. Kneeling behind the overturned sled, Slim leveled up and fired more deliberately. The other's gun blazed, too.

Slim felt the sting of a bullet as it tore through the surface muscles of his arm. But the man on the trail, Slim saw, must be struck deeper than that, for he sagged suddenly and crumpled face forward into the snow.

Slim felt so sick and weak he thought he would keel

over. It was not his own wounds that were bothering him, but this other—look what he had done. Now, added to his crimes, was—murder! Now it *would* be the seven-times-around hemp knot for him. No escape. The Mounties would hound him to the ends of the earth.

Even while despair consumed him, the injustice of his fate rankled. All of this—it wasn't his fault. In his heart he wasn't any worse a man than he had been yesterday. Only in the eyes of man-made law was he a thief and a murderer.

That was all right if they wanted to send out a posse cross-country to cut him off. But why must they come shooting, as if he were a vicious wolf that had killed a trapper's child or something? No justice to that. Plainly their intent wasn't to capture; it was to kill.

Suddenly, Slim's eyes widened. He thought he detected a slight movement from the form slumped there in the snow. Maybe the man wasn't dead after all! If he could get him on his sled and take him somewhere to a doctor— He bounded forward.

Slipping the automatic into his mackinaw pocket, he stooped and lifted the man to his feet. Suddenly those limp muscles under his hands grew tense. What was this? Hey! The man was jerking violently back! So—not dead! Playing possum. Trying to pull a fast one.

Slim heard him laugh harshly. He made a blind grab for the man's revolver hand. The gun roared, but the bullet zugged harmlessly into the snow at their feet. Savagely, jerking and twisting, foundering in the snow, Slim grappled for the revolver.

"I've got to end this quick," Slim's half-dazed thoughts ran. "Those other buzzards will be ducking out of the pines any second, and I've got to be long gone before that."

He let go the gun with one hand. That deadly barrel

reared up. But Slim's hammer fist was rearing up, too, in a wild roundhouse for the jaw.

Square on the button, Slim's fist crashed. The gun roared at the same instant. Slim got a face full of hot powder, but no lead.

With one glance at the man's unconscious figure sprawled there in the snow, Slim lunged back to the sled. Through the pines he caught a glimpse of a moving figure. Tough break! No time to dig out of this drift now. Diving behind the overturned *komatik*, he eased the Colt out of his pocket and waited there half-buried in the snow.

Those men who had ambushed him came on slowly. There were four of them. Evidently they had not seen him dive in here. Tensely, from behind his flimsy cover, Slim watched them approach.

What to do? He was in a cold sweat about it. There were enough crimes charged against him already; he didn't want to shoot these men down. And yet, they would shoot *him* down.

His lips pressed into a firm white line, and his chisel chin thrust forward as he made his decision. The men were closing in now. It was his life or theirs. All right. He leveled up that automatic. A feverish light leaped in his eyes, but his gun hand was steady.

With blood pounding in his temples, he shot as fast as he could pull trigger. When the last shell was ejected he stood up and threw the gun away. It sank out of sight in the snow.

The scene before his eyes seemed strangely blurred. He swayed a little, standing there.

There were two men down. He hoped vaguely that they weren't killed. The other two were streaking for the pines. From far back on the trail he could hear the crack of a whip and the *yarp-yarp* of a dog team.

So they were catching up with him—that other team. Well, he'd shaken them before; he could do it again. Have to hurry, though.

Mechanically, he bent to lift that sled on the trail. He wrenched and pulled. Something seemed to snap in his side where the rifle bullet had struck. Things went black for an instant. He fought off the blackness. His hand dropped down to his side and came away wet. Hey, he must have been clipped worse than he thought! Blood clear through his mackinaw. His wounded arm was throbbing painfully, too.

Gathering all his strength, he righted the sled with one prodigious tug, and slumped across it.

He rallied enough to sing out in a loud voice:

"Gid-dap there, dogs! Hi-ya—mush along there! Gid-dap!"

The sled started, gathered speed, streaked smoothly away. He leaned back wearily, dragging the warm furs over him.

Those other dogs sounded more plainly now. There was a confusion of voices, too. That pursuing sled was close! Well, he'd be putting distance between them from now on. They'd have to stop and pick up their wounded here. That would give him a good lead.

His white lips formed into a grim smile. Boy, he'd teach 'em things if they followed him long enough. Send ahead a posse, would they, to ambush him, shoot him down in cold blood? Well, wait till they saw how he treated posses!

Gosh, but his side hurt! That blackness with its swirling brilliants rushed over him again. He gritted his teeth, but he couldn't seem to fight it off this time. Well, he needed a rest. Good old dogs—they'd pull him through.

"Gid-dap, dogs! Mush—gid—"

His head fell back as consciousness slipped away.

When Slim came to, he found himself in a room. There was lamp light which hurt his eyes when he tried to open them. He had an impression of a lot of men crowding around. Some one was doing things to his side where the rifle bullet had struck.

A stern voice reached his ears as though from a long way off.

"He's a tough one, constable. This young desperado's coming around now."

"Sure glad to hear it, doc," a hard voice answered. "I wouldn't want to see him go out this way. There's more fittin' deaths for his kind."

Slim shuddered, and opened his eyes wide. A man, grim of face, was bending over him. That Norfolk jacket—the Mounted Police!

Another man pushed forward and grasped Slim's shoulders. He questioned in a crisp voice:

"Can you talk now?"

Slim nodded dully.

"Good. I'm the superintendent of the Canadian Exploration Company's mine here. I'll say one thing for you, young fellow: you're some driver. Schmidt got a hell-for-leather dog man this time. Where'd you learn to drive like that?"

Slim's brow wrinkled. What was this, some kind of a joke?

The superintendent spoke again, clipping his words.

"The constable picked you up on the trail outside the camp here when you weren't due to be halfway to the Forks. You must have had war. You're shot up. Your sled looks like a sieve. And one of your dogs has a flesh wound. Why didn't you wait at the Forks for your escort? Didn't you understand that the constable was to meet you there? It was a damn fool thing to do, young fellow—coming on alone. But you've got nerve, I'll say that. Let me be the first to congratulate you on bringing through this currency."

The superintendent indicated a leather satchel. Slim recognized it as the one which had been on the sled. There was a bullet hole through it now.

Slim's eyes blinked fast. What was this? The dog train had ended up at the right place? And these people didn't know? They thought he was the hired driver? His hopes soared, then fell. Long before he could get out of here, that other sled would be in, bringing the lurid facts. He might as well get it over with right now.

He blurted:

"I dropped three men back there." His voice rose and he struggled to sit up. "I had to shoot 'em. I had to!"

"Take it easy, young fellow." The lean-faced superintendent smiled. "Look here, did you notice—was one of them wearing a bearskin parka? Big fellow with a black bearskin—"

Slim nodded. "He was the first one I got."

There was a stir in the room.

"Black Bruele!" the constable exploded. "You shot Black Bruele! And two more of 'em besides? Then you just about cleaned up that whole, cut-throat gang single-handed!"

Slim gulped. A great weight seemed to be lifting from him. He smiled faintly. So that wasn't a posse he had mixed it with. It was none other than Black Bruele's outlaw gang!

The superintendent was leaning forward. "There'll be rewards, of course. But we're hoping the money won't influence you to leave. As a starter we'd like to offer you a steady job driving for us."

"I don't think old Doughball would be so keen about

that." Slim sketched the high points of his departure from Caribou Bend.

The superintendent interrupted. His eyes were twinkling.

"Maybe you don't know it, but you made a record run! Don't tell *me* you can't drive. And don't let—Doughball worry you, son. I hired him. And now I want to hire you. How about it!"

"I'm hired," Slim told him happily.

Traitor of the
Natchez Trace

DANNY DOW HEARD the crackling in the cane even before the man on the shaggy horse lunged out to bar the
way. Danny pulled in on his stocky Spanish pony and
waited, tight-lipped, his gray eyes cool, while the man
from the woods walked his horse closer on the trail.

Sunlight dribbled through the green thicket. It made
glints on the man's pistols in their saddle holsters. It
flashed wickedly from the long skinning knife in a sandal-
sheath.

The War of the Revolution was well over. Those rebels
against the King were pushing West, filtering down
through the Cumberlands, following Boon's trail. The
raw new gateway town of Knoxville boomed. It spilled half
its surging population every day onto the dim trails going
West. The whole great Valley of the Mississippi was stirring—all except the Chickasaw and Choctaw strips.

It was 500 miles through these Indian Nations on the
winding Natchez Trace—500 miles through swamp and
canebrake and wilderness desolation. Here no law had pene-
trated, and no religion. Renegade white men, crowded
from more ordered lands, found the territory a pirate's
paradise. The dark wilderness fed, clothed and hid
them—and provided them with victims in the farmers and
traders who flat-boated their season's products down the

Ohio and Mississippi rivers and came back overland with their gold.

The land-pirates robbed—and killed cruelly in order that the robberies might go unreported, in order that they might the more easily rob again. Traders who made the northward trip and arrived at Nashville *safely with their gold*, boasted about it for the rest of their lives.

Danny Dow didn't boast. But he had been riding the trail in safety every month of the year for six straight years!

He didn't carry gold though. A messenger on the Trace, he served the government on the mail route that had been established between the American settlements and the Spanish Province of Louisiana. Six years of it, and nothing that could happen in the big woods could surprise him.

That was why he sat his pony quietly when the man lunged from the canebrake and rode close. The man, Danny recognized, was Little Yellen. With his brother, Big Yellen, he had been levying on the Trace for years. No bigger than Danny, under his whisker stubble Little Yellen was swarthy as an Indian.

With animal furtiveness the outlaw's glance moved both ways on the trail, then fastened on Danny with a look of hard speculation.

"What news ye got?"

"Not much." Danny cocked a leg over the horn of his saddle and relaxed. "You know May-pole Maggy's place in Natchez-Under-the-Hill? She got burned out. Laid it onto the toffs from the bluff. They never even sent the fire department down. Maggy's gone to New Orleans."

Little Yellen's eyes, chips of blue quartz, were still roving. Danny could tell that there was something working

in that warped little possom mind. He bided his time and
tried again.

"You heard about Yazoo Nappycot? Lost his shirt in a
game of All-Fours in Baton Rouge. To a couple of keelboat
men down from Pittsburgh. You know how snortin' mad
Yazoo gets? He pitched into 'em both, swingin' a bottle.
They kilt him."

Little Yellen grunted, but his eyes remained disinter-
ested—and cunning. His hair shagged over his neck and
forehead, but in the back he wore it long in a kind of
scalp lock, with beaded horse hair braided through it. A
leather shirt, the fringes dirt-slick and curled, hung
loosely on him. He wore coarse butternut jeans and moc-
casins.

Danny gave up trying to interest him, and just waited.
Women or fights—those were the things Little Yellen usually was avid to hear about. Danny had a kind of silent
understanding with the Trace outlaws. When they stopped
him and asked him for it, he passed them out the news
of the towns. Beyond that, he left them alone and they
left him alone.

Six years of this, and it was enough to wring a man's
stomach dry. But what could you do? He didn't like frat-
ernizing with trail butchers so casual about murder they
didn't even stop to wash the blood out from under their
fingernails. But everybody wanted the mail to go through.
Then this was the price they had to pay—that their mail
carrier had polite truck with murderers.

Some of those smug ones in the towns who looked at
him askance—who were they to put on such a holy face?
They knew what was going on in these woods. Why didn't
they do something about it? Too busy grabbing for land
and chasing the almighty dollar, that was why.

Little Yellen grunted again. "I'm on the way back from a trip to the towns myself," he offered.

"Yeah? I didn't see you."

"You wasn't supposed to," Little Yellen told him coldly, then came out flat with what was bothering him. "You see anybody on the trail this mornin'? A long money-bags maybe, dried-up and oldish, wearin' a pepper 'n salt coat, and stridin' a gray mare?"

Little Yellen's lips clamped over the words, like a steel trap closing, and he leaned closer, peering.

Danny waved him back. "What do you think," he asked sharply, "that I'm scoutin' for you?"

"I asked ye a question."

"And I give you the answer. I'm like the Chinese monkey. On this trail I see nothin', hear nothin', tell nothin'. I go about my business—you go about yours. You know that's how it is."

"I know that's how it was. Here of late I ain't so sure."

"What you meanin' by that?"

"You won't help us. Not ever. Would you help *them* maybe? Jest once in a while maybe?" Little Yellen's lips thinned out again, straight and bloodless across his meager face. Little Yellen killed sometimes, they said, just for the fun of it.

Six years on the Trace, brushing elbows with bush-killers, had given Danny Dow plenty of assurance. The trick was never to let these fellows know you were afraid of them. Steal their thunder. It confused, then quieted them. Every time.

Danny said, "If I ever went out for helpin' *them*, I wouldn't want to let you know, would I? You'd tuck a long knife under my belt, scoop out my guts, fill my belly up with sand, and dump me in the first crick we come to, fer the eels to chew on. Ain't that right?"

Little Yellen's shoulders sank gently as he sighed. Some of the glassiness went out of his eyes. "That's right," he said. "Sure—sure. That's what I'd do." He laughed then, a laugh with plenty of noise, but no mirth.

He heeled his horse in closer, reached over and started fumbling with the straps on Danny's mail pouch.

"Hey!" Danny protested.

Little Yellen turned on him, leering. "Maybe you're carryin' gold. Maybe them eels been waitin' too long to be fed."

"You know our understandin'. I carry no gold and no gun."

"I don't know nothin' for sure," Little Yellen said flatly. "Not till I take a look for myself. Big Yellen and me talked it over before I left for the towns. It's been slim pickin's here of late. You maybe ain't to blame. But I told him I was anyhow goin' to stop you this trip and find out."

"You won't find nothin'," Danny snapped, "but some letters and some newspapers."

Little Yellen went on looking, and it was just as Danny had said. Little Yellen dumped all the mail back except one long envelope of heavy parchment paper, impressive with its ornate writing and seals of red wax.

"What's this?" he demanded.

"How do I know?" Danny growled. "It says it's from the Spanish Governor General of Louisiana, and it's addressed to the Governor of Tennessee—" He broke off, said quickly, "Hey, you can't do that!"

Little Yellen had pulled out his knife and was working the blade under the wax seals.

"Tamperin' with the U.S. mails," Danny protested again, "that's agin' the law—" He stopped, overwhelmed by his own foolishness. Law on the Natchez Trace! But some day there would be. He only hoped he lived to see the day.

With sullen concentration Little Yellen went ahead and opened the envelope. "From one Governor to another," he said, "it's liable to be somethin' concernin' how I make my livin'." Some of the glassiness came back in his eyes. "You know in Louisiana they lately hanged four our boys? Uncle Sam, he ought to go down there and clean them Spaniards up."

Little Yellen opened the letter. A look of disgust crossed his face. "It's writ in Spanish," he said.

"I could of told you that," Danny grumbled. He reached out and took the letter from the envelope before the violently unstable mind of the outlaw could dictate destruction.

Danny waited then, swallowing his anger, while Little Yellen pawed through the blanket roll behind the saddle and hefted the bag of shelled corn that Danny carried for the horse.

"All right," Little Yellen said, giving Danny a surly look, "you got a clean ticket. But maybe I'll have better luck next time."

Danny clucked to the pony, and started moving. He heard Little Yellen call after him threateningly, "You're goin' to run into Big Yellen down the trail. He'll search you too. We're goin' to be watchin' you close from here on out. We find any gold on you, and it's the knife—and eels."

Danny put the pony to a hard gallop to make up time. It was slow going at best. Unseasonable rains had softened the trail, making it a yellow quagmire. The creeks were running fast and high, lapping at the pole bridges. Places that ordinarily could be forded had to be swum.

He came out of the cane and jimson flats and into the

dark forest again, where beech and oak trees stretched shaggy arms over the trail, lifting to a height of 200 feet to blot out the sky. The silence here was something that gnawed at your mind if you let it. That was the trouble with the Trace bandits. About all of them had the bush-jumps.

All of a sudden it wasn't silent any more. A squirrel chattered, and a jay bird started a raucous clamor. A cat bird screeched, a family of wrens poured on their teeth-on-edge scolding. The disturbance centered ahead where the trail dipped to a nameless creek bed. Danny scanned the green in-bellying wall of trailside growth as he moved along.

They saw each other at about the same instant, Danny and the "long money-bags, dried-up and oldish, wearing a pepper 'n salt coat." The man appeared from behind a tangle of blackberry briars and seedling gum trees. He came, waving at Danny and climbing a clay bank, with the wet clay clinging in yellow gouts to his boots. There was more clay on his clothes. It just about covered him everywhere. He certainly was a sorry looking sight.

The man was panting when he topped the bank. "You're the mail carrier, ain't you?" he gasped, his hand lifting vaguely to indicate Danny's saddle pouch. "Been looking for you. Knowed you was due somewheres along. I'm Mot Lathrington from the Illinois country. I got held up—"

"I know," Danny interrupted. "I met Little Yellen back the trail a ways. He put you afoot?"

"No. I got my mare hid back of that spider-webbin' of wild grape and hazel scrub. I jumped her into the crick—"

Danny nodded. "You done well. Little Yellen's like a Choctaw when it comes to trackin'."

Mot Lathrington's jaw with its ridiculous stub of gray-

ing beard thrust out with decision. "Probably you could
advise me what to do. I—I'm carryin' considerable weight
of metal—"

"You're in the Devil's own fix," Danny told him. This
wasn't the first traveler who had ever appealed to him for
help. This was, in fact, an old weary story. Danny turned
in saddle, and waved behind him, down-trail. "Little Yellen's lookin' for you that way." He looked back and waved
up-trail. "*Big* Yellen, I happen to know, is holed in somewheres up ahead. With the woods so wet, and runnin'
out to low land and swamps on both sides, you got no
choice but to stick to the trail. I ain't tryin' to scare you.
Just givin' you the size."

"But there must be some way—"

"You could bury your gold, and try ridin' along with
me. If you ain't packin' gold you got a chance. Later you
could try coming back for your gold when the woods are
dried out, so's you can work across country when you
have to, off the trail."

Mot Lathrington shook his head. "That'd be too late."

Danny shrugged. "How come you're ridin' alone anyhow? You should of waited for a party to make up."

"I know. But I was in a hurry—and I didn't think the
Trace could be as lawless as they said."

"Hardly no one does," Danny said dryly. "That's why
things can go on like this year after year. The ones who
could tell are mostly dead and belly-weighted in crick
mud."

"I—I got to get my gold through," Mot Lathrington said
desperately.

"I hope you make it, friend," Danny told him. "If you
do, maybe you'll try stirrin' the government to doin' something. A disgrace and blot on the stars and stripes, that's
what it is. The Spaniards protect their part of the trail

from Natchez into New Orleans. Why can't Uncle Sam string out a few soldiers between Natchez and Nashville?" Danny's voice was rising. This was something that had been bitterly on his mind for a long time. "I'll tell you why. Too many politicians in too many county courthouses, soft-squattin' in cane-bottomed chairs and spittin' tobacco juice in brass spittoons. They just can't be bothered."

The traveler was looking at Danny in close speculation. "I've heard it said the outlaws never bother you."

"You insinuatin'?" Danny bristled.

"Just remarkin'," Lathrington said meekly. "I was thinkin' if you know them, you could take my gold through for me. I'd be glad to pay you whatever—"

"Not a chance. Be glad to do it for nothin', but they've got suspicious of me here of late. Little Yellen stopped and searched me this mornin'. His brother is bound to do the same farther along the trail." His voice rose bitterly again. "There's plenty of folks thinks my appeasin' of the outlaws extends to active collaboration with 'em. It ain't so. I do my job, that's all. I carry the mail."

Lathrington started pleading then. "Why I got to get the gold through," he said, "it ain't all mine. There was seven of us signed papers to the Wabash and Western Land Development Co., and took up land on the Wabash River in the Illinois country. We been five years breakin' our backs clearin' that land, half starvin' our wives and children the meanwhile.

"Last year we had our first sizable crops. We pooled together, and they elected me to flatboat everything down river to New Orleans. Now I got to get home with the gold. I got to get home fast. If I don't, the Land Company takes the land back. You see, they're sharpers. They get the land cleared this way for nothin'. When we first sign their papers they know it's goin' to be nigh impossible for us to meet their agreement. But we don't know that—not till too late—"

Danny sighed. There was nothing new about the story. It was happening all over the West. Thieves worked inside the law as well as outside of it, as the settlers swarmed in, eager and unwary, heeding only the call of the new land.

"All right," Danny said wearily, "I'll see what I can do to get your gold through for you. But how the hell am I going to work it? My blanket roll, the feed bag, the mail sack—no other places to hide it, and all three are bound to get searched." He lifted his glance moodily from the yellow clay bank. His grin was thin and wolfish. "Maybe I got an idea. You heard about the time not so long back that a posse caught up with a river pirate they called Charlie Busha? They got him just in under the Tennessee line, and they brought his head back inside of a big ball of clay in order to preserve same and prove up for the bounty that was put on Charlie Busha."

"I heard about it," Mot Lathrington said.

"So did Big Yellen," Danny said tightly. "He knowed Charlie Busha. All right, what do you reckon Big Yellen would think if he stopped us and seen a big ball of clay inside my mail bag, with maybe a letter tied onto it from the Governor of Louisiana addressed to the Governor of Tennessee?"

The breath caught in Mot Lathrington's throat. "He'd figger it was another head, wouldn't he? That on the Spanish side they'd captured some desperado wanted on this side, and was sendin' the head up here for proof!"

Danny nodded.

"But instead of a head, it'd be my gold inside the clay ball!"

Danny looked at the traveler steadily. "How's it strike you?"

"Might work—if he only *looked* at the clay ball. But what if he picked it up? I'm carryin' a heavy poke. He could tell by the weight—"

"I thought of that too. So it's no good puttin' the gold in the clay ball. We'll just have to put it somewhere like inside my blanket roll—and use the clay ball for a blind, try to get Big Yellen so curious about it that he'll forget to look any farther for the gold."

"Purty big risk, ain't it?"

"You know any better way?"

"No," Lathrington said ruefully, "I don't."

"Then let's get started. While I work up the clay ball, you go back along the trail a little ways and cover for me. It's just possible that Little Yellen has took a notion in that shake-brained possom head of his'n to start back in this direction. He's due to join Big Yellen up ahead here somewheres, and it could just as well be sooner as later."

It was sooner!

Danny put his pony down the bank, and was building up his ball out of clay that was firm enough to work, and still would hold its shape, kneading in some sticks and leaves for reinforcement, when his bush-wise ears heard the soft pounding of hoofs on the trail. He dropped his work and turned to peer through the creekside tangle of undergrowth. Trumpet creeper, whortleberry, and wild plum scrub reached out to tear at his clothes, and he was still fighting his way through the green thicket when he heard the two pistol shots.

The echoes rolled soddenly through the bush, stark, portentous, squeezing the waiting menace of the wilderness into one high moment of realization, as when an animal screams in the dark. Sweating, muddy, bleeding from briar scratches, Danny got clear of the leafy fingers which bound him. He broke out onto the trail, and there was one dead man, and it was Little Yellen.

"What happened?" Danny demanded, running forward.

Mot Lathrington, dried up, lank, clay-plastered, and scared looking, was standing there, his pistol loose in his dangling hand.

He looked dazedly at Danny. "He come along just like you was afeered he might. I—I braced him. He shot first. He missed. I didn't."

Danny rubbed at his jaw, looking at this old farmer with bright interest. "Friend, I don't mind sayin' I'm impressed."

Lathrington looked as though he, too, was overcome by his own deed. "He must of killed maybe a hundred men in his time."

Danny was looking in hard judgment at the body of Little Yellen huddled in the mud. "He sure is peaceful now, ain't he?" He turned to the traveler. "If there was more men of your speerit ridin' this trail, there'd be less like him."

"Then you ain't mad at me?" Mot Lathrington asked anxiously. "This dead man wasn't even a—a left-handed kind of friend of yourn?"

Danny's weathered face turned a dull brick red. "Ain't you never goin' to get that idea out of your head?" he said angrily. "You and everybody thinks on account I know a lot of these fellas by their front names, that I likewise consort with 'em—and maybe featherin' up my nest for my old age out of their blood money. What I do, I do so's the mail can go through. It ain't my shame. It's the public's—and the government's."

"Fergit I said anything," Mot Lathrington pleaded.

Danny quieted down. "It's all right," he said. "It's only that I've got to buck that kind of suspicionin' at towns both ends of my route. No matter; give me a hand with the carcass and we'll heave it into the crick."

"What'll we do about his horse?"

"Take the bit out of his mouth and leave him forage. He won't range far. Some traveler will some time pick him up."

Together they carried the body of Little Yellen, but when they were swinging it for the heave over the creek bank, Danny said sharply, "Wait a minute! I got another idea."

They lowered the body into the clay at their feet. In growing excitement Danny said, "It's an idea how to make our story stick stronger with Big Yellen when we meet him and he starts askin' questions about the clay ball we'll be carryin'."

Danny reached to grasp the scalp lock of Little Yellen's braided hair. The outlaw's head lolled under Danny's hands, and Danny's eyes glowed with such hard speculation that Mot Lathrington stirred nervously and said in a shocked voice:

"You don't mean you aim to put this hold-up fella's head *for real* inside the clay?"

"No, no," Danny said, "not the head—just the scalp lock. Think a minute. What would Big Yellen do if he seen this hair stickin' out of the clay ball? He'd get so excited, wouldn't he, that he never would think to search through the rest of my gear for the gold?"

Mot Lothrington's Adam's-apple went up and down on his skinny neck as he swallowed in apprehension. "He might forget about lookin' for the gold, but he'd haul off and kill us both, wouldn't he, if he cotched us with what he thought was his brother's head?"

"He ain't goin' to think it's his brother's head. He's goin' to think it's his own."

"His own head in the clay? You daft or what?"

Lathrington watched with growing distrust and worry as Danny got up and scrimmed around and came back with two small pieces of rock. There were a few glass beads strung on the horsehair that bound Little Yellen's hair in its braided lock. What Danny did was take the ornamental beads between the two pieces of rock and break them one by one. Then with Little Yellen's own knife he cut the lock off close to the head. He rolled Little Yellen's body off the creek bank then, and watched the water suck and pull as the flood current towed its burden into deep-woods oblivion.

After Danny had finished impressing the hair-lock in the clay ball, he stood back and viewed his handiwork, explaining, "Big Yellen wears his hair the same way Little Yellen did. With one difference. He never put none of them milky-blue beads in it. So you see what we got? From the looks of it outside, it could be Big Yellen's head in the ball."

"Yes, but—"

Danny moved over to his pony and reached inside the mail pouch. He brought out the long envelope from the Spanish Governor General of the Province of Louisiana. He opened it and spread out the letter for Mot Lathrington to examine closely.

"I got to carry ink and a quill for folks to sign for mail I deliver." Danny's fingers traced the open half-line spaces between paragraphs in the letter. "Plenty of room for writin' in Big Yellen's name in places. Now you see what I'm drivin' at? Big Yellen can't read Spanish no more than what we can. But he can read English a little. When he sees his name all through this letter, he'll naturally conclusion that the Spanish Governor General is talkin' about him and his head—"

"But this Big Yellen," Lathrington protested dazedly, "will know his own head can't be two places at once, on his shoulders and in this ball of clay—"

That wolf grin shown on Danny's face again. "That's just the point," he said. "He'll figure they've captured somebody on the Spanish side that they've mistook for *him*. He'll figure he's got the joke on two separate governors. If I know Big Yellen right, he'll laugh so much he'll entire forget to finish searchin' us."

Mot Lathrington nodded in excited appreciation. But then he sobered down. "Tamperin' with the U.S. mails— that's considerable of a crime, ain't it? Especially a Governor's letter!"

"You leave me worry about that," Danny growled. "The Governor of Tennessee will be some puzzled to see Big Yellen's name all through the letter. But whatever is writ in Spanish will still be there. . . . Now I got to go look for some sticky milkweed to stick these seals back in place again so Big Yellen'll never know we opened the envelope."

They rode all the rest of that day and a part of the next morning, with the deep woods breathing its silent menace always. "When it happens," Danny predicted, "it'll likely be in a canebrake. Wildcats, snakes, and outlaws—they all hant the canebrakes."

Danny wasn't wrong. At a place where the trail was hedged in by cane so dense that the eye could penetrate no more than ten feet, Big Yellen appeared to bar the way—Big Yellen and three other long-haired bushies who commonly trailed with him. Danny knew them all by sight. One, a cheek-scarred grizzly, Milt Yancy, he knew by name.

Danny played the same kind of game he had with Little Yellen the day before. "Howdy, boys," he greeted, and slumped in his saddle, letting them ride close.

"Who's he?" Big Yellen poked a dirt-slick thumb in the direction of Mot Lathrington.

Danny had a story ready. "He's a U.S. Mail inspector ridin' the Trace with me this trip."

"Seems like," Big Yellen said with heavy suspicion, "there's been a awful heap of inspectin' the last year or so. I been leavin' you get by with that story on the others. This one I'm dressin' down."

"Sure," Danny said agreeably. "Look him over. In your business a fella can't be too careful."

"You damn right, he can't. While I'm about it, I'm lookin' you over too."

"Help yourself," Danny said. "I got lots of time."

Big Yellen stared sullenly. Except that he was bigger, he was a dead ringer for his brother. The same black hair tied in the Indian braid. The same animal furtiveness. The sharp nose and mean little eyes, and thin lips making a straight slash across his face and nearly buried in whisker stubble.

"You see Little Yellen?" he demanded.

Danny nodded. "He stopped me yesterday in the cane t'other side Nansco's Lick."

"It's a good thing you never lied to me," Big Yellen said, his eyes flat and glassy. "I knowed you seen him, on account he said he was goin' to time his trip up from the Spanish side so's he could check on you."

"He didn't find nothin'," Danny said. "Neither will you. I'd be a fool to try to pack gold past you. Think I want your knife—and eels?"

"You'll git 'em," Big Yellen threatened, "the first time you try to put anything past me." His grimy hand lifted to scowling Milt Yancy, hulking in saddle beside him. "You and the boys search t'other'n. I'll take care Danny."

As he kneed his horse in close and reached for the strap on the mail pouch, Danny flashed a reassuring glance at Mot Lathrington. Inside Danny's coat, stuck in his belt, was one of Mot Lathrington's pistols. Mot, himself, had kept the other. If things came to the worst, they each had one bullet to shoot. Two bullets against four!

The odds, Danny reflected starkly, weren't even as good as that. Old farmer Lathrington had been lucky, that was all, when he dropped Little Yellen yesterday. That kind of lightning-luck didn't hit twice, so if it came to a showdown it was Danny Dow on his own. Against these four who lived with murder he wouldn't have the chance of a sick rabbit in a hound pack.

Well, no reason to think it might come to a showdown. He had planned for this moment inside and out. He said now:

"Ain't you wantin' to hear the news of the towns? There's a good story goin' around 'bout Mike Fink and a wrestlin' bear. On Stack Island it was, and true they say—"

But Yellen cut him short. "Little's due in here today or tomorrow," he growled. He always called his brother "Little." That was all, just "Little." Of all things on earth Little Yellen was probably the only thing that could strike a spark of human sentiment from Big Yellen. "Little's jus' been to the towns. He'll tell me all I need to know."

He had the pouch open now, and was pulling at the moss which Danny had plastered onto the clay ball.

"What the hell's that?"

"What's it look like?"

"Ball o' clay."

Danny nodded. "That's what I was told when I signed

for it in the Post Office at Natchez, and I had no call to
doubt it."

"It's still damp."

Danny looked bored. "My instructions calls for keepin'
it that way. Clay preserves better damp. Every night I
sprinkle some water on it."

Big Yellen yanked the pouch around so the sun would
shine in. He caught hold of the braided lock of hair stick-
ing out of the ball with the long envelope fastened to it.
He looked at Danny with heavy-lidded suspicion.

"What's inside that clay ball?"

"Just what you're thinkin'."

"A head—like Charlie Busha that time?"

"Like Charlie Busha," Danny said.

The others had quit their searching of Mot Lathrington's trail-gear now, and were looking over, interested. A
tension grew upon them all.

"What you sweatin' for?" Big Yellen asked Danny.

"Hot," Danny said.

"Who's head is it?"

Danny shrugged. "They never said."

"Got hair like mine."

"Don't prove nothin'. Every here and there in the bush
you run acrost a fella wearin' it that way."

Big Yellen pulled the envelope free from the hair. He
squinted at it for a long time in the sun. "It's from the
Spanish Governor General of Louisiana," he said, and he
sounded impressed. "He's sendin' the head to the Governor of Tennessee."

Danny nodded. "What I figure, it's somebody that's
wanted bad on this side, that they've cotched down under
the line. Must be somebody awful important for 'em to go
to so much trouble."

Sunlight glinted on bright steel as Big Yellen whipped

out a knife and started prying at the red wax that bore the Governor's seal, precisely as Little Yellen had done the day before.

It was history repeating itself all around, because Danny said sharply, "Hey, you can't do that! Tamperin' with the mails—there's a law—"

But Big Yellen was already doing it. He unfolded the letter and held it between his dirt-greased hands. His mean little eyes blinked as the sun struck the white paper. He looked up.

"It's writ in Spanish," he said, in disgust.

"Sure," Danny said, "what'd you think?"

But Big Yellen was looking at the letter again. Suddenly he let out a whoop and started laughing. He slapped at his jean-clad thigh—and kept on laughing. His men were staring. So was Danny, who put on a good act, pretending he didn't know what in the world had got into Big Yellen.

Big Yellen calmed down enough at last to hold up the letter and prod at it with his fingers. "Look," he said, "look. It's writ in Spanish, but I can read *my* name in it, all through it everywhere. *Big Yellen*, it says!" He shook the paper. "Don't you see what that means? The Governor thinks he's got *my* head in that ball o' clay! He's cotched some rovin' woods gunner, and he's mistook him fer me, more'n like on account of the hair. He thinks he's cotched me, and he's makin' the Governor o' Tennessee a present of my head! That there sure is a handsome joke on a couple o' Governors!"

He started laughing again—and this time everybody else was laughing with him. This was working out all right, Danny told himself tensely, and he swapped a quick glance with Mot Lathrington. They were as good as on their way now—with Big Yellen's blessing. Their hides were safe, and so was the gold. Why, it wouldn't be too surprising if Big Yellen even passed around a jug of his Monongahela whiskey.

Then, as suddenly as he had begun, Big Yellen quit laughing. He had yanked the ball of clay half out of the pouch and was examining the hair. He bent to look closer. Danny looked too.

Alarm stabbed through him. It coursed his whole nerve-taut body and tingled his toes. Big Yellen was pinching at some dried clay that was stuck to the hair. When Danny had cracked the beads between the two pieces of rock, he had taken pains to shake the hair and blow at it, to rid it of the shattered bead fragments. But now he could see the tiny splinter of milky-blue glass that was impressed in the clay. The splinter wasn't the only thing.

Big Yellen looked up, his eyes naked with dark hatred. "Somethin' you never knowed—that Little and me put different knots in the horse hair we used to fasten our scalp locks with. This here is Little's knot. That's a sliver of Little's beads in the clay. This here is Little's hair! . . . *You never took it offen him alive.*"

Danny was doing his despairing best to wrestle the pistol from under his coat. But he was a mile and a rod too slow, and he knew it. Big Yellen's knife hand had already started its lightning strike.

So after all it was the knife—and eels, Danny thought starkly—with no one outside the big woods knowing, with everyone forever continuing to think that Danny Dow was tainted with the outlaw brand. "*I knew he'd get it some day,*" the wiseacres would say. "*When thieves fall out—*"

Then the pistol shot laid its close echoes flatly across the trail. The knife of Big Yellen fell short of Danny's stomach, raking down to gash the leather mail pouch . . . and Big Yellen pitched from saddle between the horses, his face contorted in its death spasm.

That high-pitched scream of triumph was the old farmer's! Mot Lathrington had scored again. First Little Yellen. Now Big Yellen. Unbelievable! But the evidence was here in Big Yellen's bullet-weighted body.

The next shot came from that scarred grizzly, Milt Yancy. Danny didn't feel anything, so he figured that the bullet must have reached out for the farmer. Danny had his own pistol in the clear now. The big hammer snapped down, the barrel spit ball and powder—and Milt Yancy, in the act of drawing his second pistol, doubled over in saddle and slipped off sidewise to thump in the mud beside Big Yellen.

The horses were rearing, and the other two outlaws were putting more lead in the air—deadly close-in firing, so close that Danny felt the spit of powder on his face and caught the reek of gun smoke in his nostrils. He couldn't tell if he was hit or not. But he was still in saddle. And so was the farmer.

Danny struck out with his empty pistol, leaning from saddle and bringing his arm down with all its tensioned strength. The force of the blow knocked the pistol from his hand—but the man who had the long barrel laid across his head was knocked from his horse too.

From the tail of his eye Danny saw the farmer and the last one of the outlaws tumble from their horses, locked in savage embrace. He went off his horse in a sprawling leap—but before he could reach the farmer to help him, the farmer helped himself. Amazingly, he pulled out of the fighting grapple and stood up. He had a knife in his hand and there was blood on the blade. The outlaw never did stir after that. Neither did the one that Danny had knocked from saddle.

Danny's eyes swept fiercely from the four dead men to the farmer. "You all right?" he called hoarsely.

Mot Lathrington was shaking himself. "Seems like."
"Me too," Danny said between breaths, but he still
didn't quite believe it.

A little later, sitting in the mud, resting, Danny wiped
sweat and batted at gnats—and accepted a fill for his
pipe from Mot Lathrington's pouch of home-cured rough-
cut.

"What riles me," Danny complained, "is we can't take
credit for this with the public. Not if the mail's goin' to
keep goin' through. News of what we done has got to stay
buried in this canebrake, so's I can keep appeasin' the
rest of the outlaws still levyin' on the Trace."

"You sound uncommon bitter," Mot Lathrington said.

"Wouldn't you be?" Danny flared. "Only half trusted
by outlaws and honest men alike. All because of the—"

"The politicians spittin' in the brass spittoons, and the
land grabbers too busy with chasin' the almighty dollar.
That the way of it?"

"Yeah," Danny said, then he noticed Mot Lathrington's
sly peculiar smile. There was a question that had been
burning in Danny from the first. "Where'd you learn to
fight so good?" he demanded.

"Fightin's my business, son."

"Huh? I thought farmin' was."

"I was bound to tell you that."

Danny's pipe went unregarded in his hand. "Hey,
what's goin' on here?"

"You come close to it with what you told Big Yellen."

"I told him you was ridin' the Trace with me, as a U.S.
Mail inspector."

Mot Lathrington nodded. "The Post Office Department
did hire me—"

"Huh? For what?"

"To check on you mostly."

Danny was staring now with his jaw sagging. What he was thinking about particularly was the scandalous way he had tampered with the mail entrusted to his charge—*in front of an inspector.*

Mot Lathrington was talking again. It turned out to be quite a speech he made. "You're right about one thing, son. It is a shame and a crime how the government has left this mail route to limp along and take care of itself. But in a big country like ours, new and growin', it takes time to get around to meetin' all the needs. Meanwhile the mail's got to somehow go through, and to accomplish that—" Mot Lathrington pulled at his pipe—"the carrier's has got to be like you, honest, brave, resourceful, and with a knack for stayin' alive until such time as fightin' can begin. You see, there's been tall tales circulatin' through the department about you—tall tales, good and bad." He smiled warmly. "Now I can go back and tell 'em the good ones is the true ones."

Danny took a deep breath and looked both ways on the trail self-consciously. "We better start roundin' up the horses."

"No hurry, is there?"

"But your gold—"

"You didn't see none, did you?"

Mot Lathrington was smiling in that mischievous way again.

"Course I never seen it," Danny said. "You got it sewed up tight inside the skin poke."

"It's only rifle lead inside the poke, son. Sorry how I deceived you, but my orders about puttin' you to the test called for bein' as realistic as I could. Since the lead's already here though, you might's well put it by, against that day when Uncle Sammy starts proceedin's to make the Natchez Trace as safe a place for travelers as what the highroad is between New York and Philadelphia."

Eyes glowing, Danny asked, "When's that day comin'?"

"Depends most-part on you."

"On me!"

"Sure. Six years of goin' and comin' on the Trace, and you're the one that's fitted to say. Ain't I told you? You're comin' back to Washington with me to advise the big augers on how and when and where."

Torture Trek

THREE MEN RODE into Moonstone that day. The first attracted no more attention in the sleepy mining camp than one of the dust devils blowing in a lazy whirl across the street. Strap Vernon was his name, but that didn't matter. Young, lean, and desert-browned—but none of that mattered either. Not at the start.

When he hitched his tired paint pony in front of the Fandango Saloon and drifted in through the swinging doors, the Fandango wise ones sized him up for just another gold-bitten bum in from a color trail. And they were right.

They were right about the second man, too.

He created more of a stir than the first. But that was only because of his horse. The second man was little, but his horse was huge. A strawberry roan, a magnificent animal.

Big horse—little, shriveled old man. Under his dusty sombrero he looked as though the best part of him had been blown away by desert winds, and the rest dried to a husk by the desert sun. But his eyes were bright. A clear, deep blue, the old man's eyes were something to notice and remember.

He tied his big strawberry roan next to the paint pony at the rack, pushed through the bat wings and made a place for himself beside young Strap Vernon at the bar.

The bartender looked him over. "Well, I'm a shovel-nose wolf, one of the Bonanza twins, ain't it? I couldn't

tell which one fer sure till you come out from under some
of that sagebrush."

The little man grinned. "Bonanza Bill, that's me. Year
ago to a day I was in here with brother Bob. Mebbe you
recollect he went one way and I went tother. We was each
to scrounge the desert fer a year and meet back here where
we started from. I'm waitin' fer him now."

"You get any gold?" the bartender asked.

"Naw." Bonanza Bill shrugged his thin shoulders. His
face was cheerful. "No gold. But I got me that strawberry
roan out yonder. I always wanted a good horse. All my
life. Now I got him."

From the eminence of his steady job and his recognized
niche in a settled community, the bartender proceeded to
moralize. "All you burro bums gimme a laugh. You spend
your life kickin' rock in a desert, and if you do happen
to turn up a little color, what do you do? Provide for your
future? No. You soak your wad on somethin' like a elegant
horse that you don't need."

"Who says I don't need a good horse?"

"What you need him for?"

"Fer . . . fer my happiness," the old man said defen-
sively. "Hell's hoptoads, you ain't tellin' me nothin', young
feller. All your hollerin' about the future is hogwash.
Comes a time in a man's life when he sees plain that his
future's plumb sloshed out over the rim of his gold pan.
All he's got is the present, and if he's smart he settles fer
somethin' he's been wantin' for a long time. Hell's hoptoads, gimme a drink!"

Strap Vernon shouldered closer to the oldster and
grinned. "I like how you talk, mister. Leave me to buy
the drinks."

Bonanza Bill stared at him from under his white brows,
grayed now with desert dust. "Thanks, bub, thanks," he

said. "My brother ought to be along almost immediate. He's like to have a poke of gold that'll leave us buy the whole dang saloon."

The bartender threw up his hands. "There he goes. Moans about he ain't got no future. Now he's gonna buy the Fandango."

That one raised a friendly laugh all around and the bartender, grinning, poured out drinks.

"Reckon we better drink to this flea-bit town of Moonstone," said Bonanza Bill. "Shore looks like it needed encouragement."

"Diggin's is peterin' out fast," a miner volunteered. "Any half-necked strike within a thousand miles, and Moonstone'd be emptied before night."

The way it turned out, the miner was right as rain in a dry month, because almost before the prediction had left his lips the green-shuttered doors fanned air for a third time and let in one more newcomer.

The Fandango wise ones were a mile and a rod off in their estimate of this third man. He was a tall, lank, cadaverous individual with loose-jowled face and flat, staring eyes. He had on a brand-new outfit—high-crowned derby, stand-up collar, short sack coat over a green checkered vest, and tight pants.

He didn't utter a word, just reached carefully inside the sack coat and pulled out a .45-caliber hogleg, leveled off calmly and sunk one shot—in the middle of the big bar mirror.

Gunshot echoes rolled under the low ceiling, and the crashing jangle of broken glass was loud in every ear. Still the man didn't say anything. But while the early-morning bar loungers stared frozen-faced, he did make a sound.

It was a kind of inarticulate yip deep in his throat. Excitement effects men in odd ways. This hombre simply squeezed that funny noise from his dead-pan face and threw his arm up once in a short jerky movement. Then he carefully put his six-gun away and smoothed his sack coat over the bulge.

The bartender showed his excitement in a more conventional manner. "You blank-faced, locoed, double-distilled idiot," he blared, "you know what that'll cost you?" He named the first number that came to his mind. "Five hundred dollars." His hand reached under the bar for the hide-away six-gun. "Lay it on the line, mister. Five hundred dollars."

The stranger, still showing all the radiant animation of a dried buffalo chip, walked over to the bar and shoved his hand in the pocket of his sack coat. Men close to him could see the hand trembling now and the loose jowls twitching, and they knew that in spite of the easy act he was putting on, his nerves were tight as a newly stretched fence.

His hand pulled out of his pocket and jerked toward the bar. There was a small clatter of solid clinking sound as the fistful of irregularly shaped rocks hit and slid across the cherry wood.

Rocks? The sun, slanting feebly through the dingy windows up front, lighted up the objects, made them glow— a warm cornmeal yellow.

"Gold!" The word jumped from the throat of practically every man there.

The stranger spoke then. "Reckon that'll pay for your glass," he said coolly.

"Yeah," the bartender gasped, his pudgy hands reaching to scoop the nuggets.

He didn't get all of them. Men pushed the bar loose from its wooden-pin moorings as they flung against it, hands outstretched and grabbing.

Bonanza Bill got one of the nuggets. He turned it over in his flinty fingers, his blue eyes keenly examining its ragged shape—pure gold, worn free from its quartz matrix. Washed out of the vein, down the slope, how many ages ago? And where? It was the where that mattered. Brought to light by this cadaverous stranger from some buried creek bottom. Where?

Bonanza Bill lifted his hand up and down to feel the solid weight of the nugget. "I can't no ways identify it," he remarked.

"Neither can anyone else," the stranger said hoarsely.

"New find?" Strap Vernon asked.

"New find."

"Drinks are on the house!" the bartender bawled. "Drink to Mr.—Mr.—" He looked beseechingly at the stranger.

"Demeree Voy," the man supplied, bowing in his tight new pants and sack coat with just the right suggestion of grandeur. He was loosening up a little now, settling down to enjoy himself. He had something they all wanted and he'd give it to them, but he'd let them fawn around and lick his boots for a while first.

Before the second round of drinks was flowing the word had gone around outside, and the Fandango was jammed front to back with milling, glint-eyed men.

No one asked the question. It wasn't etiquette. But they waited, jabbering, throats dry and hearts pounding while Demeree Voy preened and strutted. Anyone with half a glance could see he wasn't the kind that men would ordinarily warm to, and all understood vaguely that he was stretching out his moment of triumph to the fullest.

So they waited and finally Demeree Voy slapped his glass on the bar and said casually, "It was in the Sundag Range."

Men took up the word. It washed around the big room in a single wave and ended in a hush. Two hundred men were crowded in that saloon, yet the drip of beer from a leaky spigot sounded plainly.

Bonanza Bill was jammed in against the great man's elbow. "There's a heap of hills in the Sundag Range," he suggested mildly.

Demeree Voy nodded. "This was on the west slope, upper end."

Like wildfire the information circulated. And again the silence clamped down.

"I been in there," said Bonanza Bill. "It still calls fer some narrerin', podner."

"I reckon," Demeree Voy agreed. But he didn't narrow down any further. Not then. Instead, he put a question. "Who owns the strawberry roan at the rack outside? Nice piece of horseflesh."

They caught on in a hurry. Men from all over the room shouted back. "*You* own him, podner."

"Like hell he does," yelled Bonanza Bill. "That's my horse and I ain't sellin'."

"You're either sellin' or givin' him away!" a dozen harsh voices beat at the old desert rat.

"Nope. Not even fer the directions to King Solomon's mines, I ain't," Bonanza Bill lashed back at them.

Demeree Voy stayed aloof from the clamor that welled about him, signaling the bartender with uplifted finger to fill his glass again.

He downed the drink and raised his hand for silence. Both the liquor and the worshipful adulation were going to his head now and he made a little speech.

"Naturally," he began, "I protected my rights by stoppin' in at the county seat and filin' my claims. But my claims only begin to touch the gold that's in that canyon.

There's gold for all, gents." He thwacked at his inside pocket. "I got a careful-drawn map that leads smack to it, and I'd admire to step outside and lead the rush to fame and fortune. But I got a hankerin' to rack off on that strawberry roan out there."

"We'll bring that hoss in here and spot him on the bar if you say so!" a miner near the bat wings said.

There was a surge through the whole crowd as a score of men boiled out through the swinging doors.

"You leave my horse alone," Bonanza Bill protested in his shrill, excited voice.

A miner popped a fist in his face. "Shut up, grandpa!"

Strap Vernon was standing close. His own fist lashed out. There was a *thup* of knuckles against jaw flesh, and the man who had struck Bonanza Bill heeled back into the crowd and would have fallen if there had been anywhere to fall.

"It's the old man's horse," Strap said angrily. "He don't have to sell if he don't want to."

Another man's fist reached in and caught Strap alongside the ear. That was the signal for a general mêlée. Strap defended himself the best he could and Bonanza Bill sided him, but with a couple hundred gold-delirious men determined to do whatever was necessary to please their parade leader, neither lasted long.

When Strap Vernon groped back to consciousness, the first thing that impressed him was the utter silence. The last he remembered fists had been thudding in and the roar of the crowd was like thunder.

Now, all about, was the silence of a tomb.

Tomb was a good name for it, he decided grimly a few moments later when awareness had flooded back sufficiently to let him look around.

His boots scuffed across a split-log floor; his hands gripped iron bars and shook. The door in its iron frame rattled. That was all—just rattled. He crossed the floor again and looked out the barred window. He was in the Moonstone jail and there wasn't a soul in sight!

He rattled the jail door again and shouted.

This time an old man's high-pitched voice answered. "I'm comin', bub."

While Strap waited, Bonanza Bill scuffed into the jail corridor. His clothes were torn, his face smeared with dried blood. Keys jangled from a loop of wire which he held in his hand. He unlocked the cell door.

"'Ceptin' us two, there ain't a man in town," Bonanza Bill said mournfully.

"Off on the gold rush, huh?"

"All of 'em. I come to on the saloon floor. My horse was gone. I took a look in the livery stable. Ain't a four-hoofed critter left in town. I was just startin' back to bust into the Fandango and anyhow help myself to some whiskey when I heard you hollerin'. The cell-door keys was in plain sight in the office. I reckon they meant me to find 'em."

"But they never meant for us to get any of the gold!" Strap swore softly. "Low-lived, maverick, horse-stealin' coyotes. With them a ridin' head start and us afoot—no use to even try."

Bonanza Bill's scrawny hand clutched at Strap's shirt. "No use fer *me* to try. But *you*—mebbe I got an idee."

"You're locoed. Where'd I find a horse in those heat-blasted Sundags? And walkin', they'd have the whole damn canyon staked out before I got halfway."

"Listen, bub, listen. I come to just before they shoved off, and previous to them fistin' me to sleep again I heard Demeree Voy slippin' the bartender special information for a price. I know almost the exact location of that strike. West slope, upper end, in the third canyon beyond Singing Rock Butte on a line with—"

"So what good is it to us?" Strap broke in impatiently. "We're here and it's there and we got no way to get there."

Bonanza Bill dug his other hand in Strap's shirt and shook furiously. "Listen to me, you young jackanapes, what I'm tryin' to tell you. I been all through that country. I know it like my own backyard—if I had a backyard. There's a short cut—"

"Through Diablo Sink, sure. Any fool knows that—"

"But any fool don't know about the waterholes this time of year," Bonanza Bill yelled. "Or about the pass I found through Indian Feather Canyon that everybody thinks is boxed and that lops two days off the climb of them west Sundag slopes. It's cruel travelin'. I'm an old man and I couldn't make it under forced draft, but you could. I can map it for you and on foot you could beat the whole bunch of 'em to the strike and file for you and me above and below discovery. How does it sound, bub?"

A wide grin spread over Strap's tanned young face. "Sounds like the clink of gold in my ears, old-timer."

Through Diablo Sink, where the sun was like a flame against the face, and the sands shriveled boot leather, young Strap Vernon forged on, pitting his youthful strength and an old man's wisdom against desert death.

With his canteens long since empty and flopping, a dead weight against his sides, he had to resist an almost uncontrollable impulse to throw them away.

The hot sands sucked at his boots with every lunging step, draining his strength as the sun drained moisture from his body. His clothes were crusted white in the creases from the salt of body sweat. His mouth seemed choked with cotton. The trail he made as he staggered on through the cruel sands was so crooked a sidewinder would have had difficulty following it.

He was a fool, he told himself, to dare Diablo Sink at this time of year. Fool . . . fool . . . fool. The word beat like a dry rattle in his brain, with every torturing step.

A fool—but only the fools found gold. He kept reminding himself of that. And in the end his young strength and the old man's desert savvy prevailed. Strap Vernon reeled into a crumble-rock draw, more dead than alive, but still on his feet. And there, just as the old desert rat had told him it would be, was water!

He dropped down and buried his face in the shallow pool, taking spare sips of the life-giving water at first, and reveling in its wet warmth. After a while he lay back to rest briefly in the shade of a tiny-leafed mesquite.

He had completed the worst of his journey. He was already in the lower benches of the Sundags. The rest of it was a matter of time and energy. He would arrive at the gold canyon first. He would beat all those who had left him behind and stampeded by saddle and buckboard.

His young strength came flowing back. He listened to the desert wind blowing in sear blasts over the scorched wasteland, and it seemed to him a good sound now.

Suddenly he sat up. A sound had come to him, borne on the wind, but not of the wind. It seemed to come from a long way off—a kind of moaning.

He whipped to his feet, plunged in among the stunted mesquite, took only a half dozen steps in all, then stopped. It wasn't a loud sound brought by the wind from a distance; it was a very low moan that came from close by.

At first sight Strap thought the gray-haired man he looked at couldn't possibly be alive. Huddled in its rags

among the rocks, the frail thin body looked too utterly
defenseless to contain any spark of life.

The man was alive though; and Strap tended him, moving him gently to the pool and bathing his bruised head
and battered body. Some of the injuries were deep; the
pathetic little wisp of a man looked as though he might
have crawled out from under an avalanche. He was burning up with fever and kept muttering incoherently as Strap
bandaged the worst of his wounds.

After those first swift ministrations Strap sat back on
his heels, only now taking sober stock of the situation.
Here was an old man dying. Maybe he could save him.
But that would mean staying here, tending him constantly,
nursing him through the fever. And staying here long
enough for that meant he wouldn't figure at all in the race
for the gold. Before he could get there the canyon would
be staked out to its farthest rim.

Yes, if he stayed here, then his tortuous trek across the
desert at the risk of his life had all been for nothing. At
least as far as he was concerned, and maybe as far as this
old man was concerned, nothing. He couldn't be sure that
all the tending in the world could keep the shriveled old
fellow on this side of the grave.

Strap bolstered up his line of reasoning with thoughts
of Bonanza Bill, waiting for him back in Moonstone.
Didn't he have a responsibility to Bonanza Bill? Certainly.
The old codger trusted him. Couldn't let him down simply
because fate had twisted time and place to bring about
this meeting with an old desert rat who was already more
dead than alive.

This old fellow had lived out most of his life anyway.
He himself was young, was only getting well started. And
here was a chance for gold, the kind of chance that
wouldn't come again as long as he lived.

But all the time that Strap's mind seethed with this kind of reasoning, he knew what he would do. A man was dying and there was a slim chance that he could be saved, so Strap stayed and did what he could.

Blazing day when the sun poured down from the sky like molten fire turned into sickly night when the heat in the ground rushed upward. Day and night, day and night. Strap didn't keep track. What was the use? He had a job, the job of saving a man's life, and it wasn't measured by time.

Carefully Strap nurtured that spark of life. The gaunt old desert rat had moments of delirium in which he raved and tossed and looked at Strap with terror filling his eyes. But in the end he quit fighting the fever phantoms, and Strap saw that sanity had returned to his gaze.

Strap knew all at once that he had won. Though everything else about the old man still looked dead, the eyes were alive. A clear and tranquil blue they were, as an old man's eyes sometimes get when he has lived his life alone under the sky.

"Who are you?" the old fellow questioned feebly.

"I found you here," answered Strap. "I've been watching you. Take it easy. You're all right."

"I thought at first you were *him*—come back to finish what you started." A shudder coursed the frail figure, and for an instant an old terror flamed in his eyes. "But you're not *him*—you're someone else, ain't you?"

"Sure, someone else," Strap said soothingly.

The old man closed his eyes and slept. When he woke up the stars were out, points of fire in the late night coolness. Strap sat close by, near a handful of flames generated by burning mesquite roots. He broke out of his dozing when the old man stirred, and his mind jerked back to realities. He had been dreaming of gold, but now he knew he'd lost the gold.

"You saved my life," the old man murmured. He was propped feebly on his elbow, focusing those clear eyes on Strap. "You saved my life," he said again. "He left me for dead. He thought sure I'd die. I thought so, too."

"Who left you for dead?" Strap asked.

"Feller I run acrost out here, dyin'. I saved him the same like you done me. I had some nuggets. He robbed me and like to beat me to death tryin' to make me tell where more was. I didn't have any more—only them few samples I'd hid under that loose rock. Near where your foot is. Move the rock and look. Purtiest stuff you ever seen."

Strap obediently moved the rock and found half a dozen small nuggets. They glowed in the light of the fire, their peculiar irregularity throwing them into odd lights and shadows.

Strap's nerves, as a result of the sleep he had missed, weren't any too steady. Suddenly the nuggets shook together as his hand started trembling. He looked up.

"What was his name—this fella that robbed you and left you for dead?"

"I disremember," the old prospector answered. "Peculiar hombre. Walkin' bean-pole, he was, with dead-looking eyes and slack skin around the jaws. He gave me the creepin' jeepers from the first—had about as much expression on his face as a buffalo chip."

"You've called it," Strap said. "Demeree Voy!"

"That's it. I mind now—Demeree Voy."

"Did he steal a map from you, too?"

"Yes, he took a map."

Strap swore under his breath. "Demeree Voy showed

up in Moonstone with your gold and your map. He led a stampede to the diggin's. I was on my way there myself, takin' a short cut through the Sink, when I ran across you."

A speculative gleam came in the old man's eyes. "You stayed to take care of me," he said slowly, "and passed up your chance to locate. Demeree Voy'll be there now, him and all that followed him. Hell's hoptoads, Moonstone must be tetotally vacated."

"Only one man left—" Strap broke off and stared. "Hey, what's that you just said?"

"Huh? How you mean?"

"Only one other man I remember hearin' say, 'Hell's hoptoads.' An' your eyes are the same blue like his—Mister, ain't you the other of the Bonanza twins?"

The old man actually chuckled. "So you run acrost brother Bill in Moonstone? I was supposed to meet him there—but I reckon he joined the stampede with the others."

"No," Strap said. "If he ain't drunk himself to death on the Fandango's free liquor, he's still in Moonstone waitin' to hear from me. Demeree Voy stole his horse."

"So brother Bill got him a horse at last. Was it a good one?"

"Hope to tell you. Pretty a strawberry roan as you'd want to see."

"Brother Bill always wanted a good horse."

"Demeree Voy stole your brother's horse," Strap explained. "But your brother never took it lyin' down. He was the one that mapped the way for me across the Sink. I was goin' to beat the push and stake claims for the both of us."

All at once Strap's hand went slack, and the nuggets dropped with tiny pludding sounds against the rock.

What was the use of talking? Life twisted things around and knotted a fellow in strange tangles with other folks, and what did any of it matter? The main thing was, he'd had a fortune in his hands and he'd let it go. No, that wasn't the main thing. Main thing was he'd saved a man's life.

Bonanza Bob started chuckling and this time he didn't stop. Strap thought he must be showing another touch of the fever. In another minute the old coot would probably be batty again. But he wasn't, as his next words clearly revealed.

"Everything's all right, son. I'm still sittin' purty on my claim, and you and brother Bill will be spotted above and below discovery. On account why? I'll tell you. On account I wasn't big enough fool to draw that map correct for Demeree Voy. The only thing that's right about it is the mountain range. Now while the wolves is tearin' up the west slope of the Sundags, we'll proceed to file on the east slope, where the gold is!"

That was where Strap interrupted him by grabbing up the nuggets, jumping to his feet and whooping.

And that was also where Demeree Voy brought himself into the picture again. His flat, emotionless voice sounded from the shadows. "All very interestin'. I'm glad to hear the honest confession."

Strap stared, unbelieving, as from behind a rocky outcrop on the rugged desert floor, Demeree Voy came into view. Starlight glinted from the six-gun held with seeming carelessness in his hand. He still wore his high-crowned derby, tight pants, and sack coat, though they weren't as spruce-looking as they had been in the Fandango Saloon.

"If it's any consolation to you," Voy continued, "they like to lynched me when they found there wasn't any gold. Don't know's I blame 'em. It even puts *me* in a killin' temper to be fooled that way. I came ridin' back to you, takin' a wide chance I might find some information on your dead body that I'd overlooked before. Sighted your fire and came in easy. Delighted to see you ain't dead— yet." He came on and stopped across the fire from them. To Strap he said, "Ain't you the hombre we left in the Moonstone jailhouse?"

"I don't stay put very long," Strap told him.

"I've got a bullet in this six that says you do."

"You leave this young feller out of it," Bonanza Bob growled. "He don't know nothin'."

"If he don't know nothin'," said Demeree Voy, "that removes my last reason for leavin' him live."

"Now look here," Bonanza Bob pleaded, "this is a deal between you and me."

"It'll be smoother dealin' with him out of our way."

Strap had been trying to whip his numbed brain into action. Someone had certainly put a jinx on him. Here he had the world handed to him again on a gold standard, and in the same split-wink a chunk of lead threatened to blast it away. Suddenly he became aware that he was hold- ing his breath—he didn't know for how long. He gasped air and jerked his head to shake sweat from his eyes. "Wait a minute," he said.

Slowly he extended his arm, opened his hand. He held his hand almost over the fire where light from the flames would reveal the nuggets. The sweaty gold made soft glints in his palm.

He was watching Demeree Voy and holding his breath again. Voy's greedy eyes flickered momentarily toward the gold. It was all the odds Strap asked. He had shifted his weight to his right foot. Without any revealing movement of his body he brought his left foot swinging sideways into the white-hot coals of the fire.

The coals scattered in a fiery arc at Voy, and Strap followed them as the six-gun blared.

That first shot was triggered purely by reflex. Strap felt the close breath of the bullet, but not its leaden bite. The second shot pludded into the ground—and that was because Strap had rammed into the gunner, knocking down his aim. The third slug went reaching for stars, because by that time Strap had a hard hold on Demeree Voy's gun arm and was contesting desperately for ownership of the gun.

Locked in deadly embrace, they strained with muscles bulged and quivering. Demeree Voy's grip on the gun started to loosen. Then he got a foot behind Strap and tripped him. Down they crashed, with Strap underneath.

But Strap didn't stay underneath. He couldn't, with a live coal feeding into his back. He bucked, arched, as the gun blasted close to his ear, deafening him. The powder seared his skin, but the lead flattened harmlessly against rock.

In recoil from the pain of the live coal, Strap's muscles bunched. Slewing his body around, he put hard sharp pressure on Demeree Voy's wrist, forcing that six-gun muzzle inch by fatal inch inward toward Voy's own heaving chest.

Demeree Voy lost his nerve there at the last. He squalled like a stricken animal and emptied his gun in panic-stricken triggering. There were only two more loads in the cylinder. The first of the two didn't count for anything. But the last one killed him, as the gun muzzle, in the grim struggle, poked over against his heart.

The night hush closed down. From somewhere through the desert darkness sounded the faint restless nicker of a horse. Hoofbeats followed, growing louder as the horse came in for water.

Strap went over and stroked the horse soothingly as he drank.

"Demeree Voy's critter, I reckon," Bonanza Bob murmured. "We can shore use him."

"Demeree stole him from your brother," Strap told him. "And I mean your brother's eyes are gonna pop when you come ridin' in on this strawberry roan. I dunno which he hated to lose most, his chance at the gold or this horse. Now he's got 'em both."

Bonanza Bob sighed. "Looks like mebbe we're all three set to enjoy a bonanza from here on out."

White Water

A ROCKY ISLAND LOOMED through the world's-end mist, and Poleon checked the forward sweep of his canoe. By straining his eyes he could make out the warning words of the sign: *Beware This Fork—Rapides du Mort.*

Poleon beached his canoe, stepped out, climbed to the sign. His stubby hands gripped it strongly, shook, noted with satisfaction that the post was firmly embedded in its cairn of rocks. Andre, he mused, would have taunted him for his caution, arguing the sign was put there by the Mounted Police. The mounties do not blunder. Therefore, the sign continues to remain firm at its base and to point the correct way.

But in the woods Poleon took nothing on trust. Here, where the waters parted, a man had to choose which fork he would take, and choose well, or else dip his way to death. It was not true, as Andre charged and as the Mounted Police most likely supposed, that Poleon was a timid man. Cautious only, and rightly so. The animals, big and little—consider them. They tread stealthily through the woods, sniffing everything, looking everywhere, listening. And the most cautious lived the longest.

Back at the water's edge, Poleon stopped short. His eyes had perceived some minute displacement of gravel not made by his own moccasoned feet. He looked further for telltale signs which might show where a man had driven a canoe ashore. He found no signs. For a moment he stared broodingly into the waist-deep water while the witch-wind of early morning breathed about him.

He returned to the signpost. Dropping on his knees, he started removing the cairn rocks. He had to lift only a few before he could see that the rock moss had been previously broken. Not longer than yesterday, because the day before there had been rain, and the rain would have settled the sand and silt in the crevices.

There was but one thing to suppose. The mad killer whom he tracked had changed the sign to point to the wrong fork, cunningly thinking to lure his pursuers into those rapids of death.

The hair tugged at its roots on the back of Poleon's thick neck as he contemplated his narrow escape. It was known that somewhere ahead the two forks of this river joined again. It was said that the waters mated in black pools overlaid with lily pads and white lily flowers. Funeral flowers. From the time of the first fur *voyageurs* into this great lone land, no man had taken his canoe through the white-water gorge and lived to boast about it. For if by a miracle he escaped the grinding death of the rapids, he met death in the overfalls, a drop, it was said, the height of a valley spruce.

Poleon went swiftly to work again. If the madman had changed the sign to point down the wrong fork, the thing to do was change it back so that Andre and all who might come carelessly after him would not be guided down the wrong waterway.

Afloat again, Poleon paddled strongly to make up for his loss of time. It was Poleon's self-appointed chore to track down this madman, to apprehend him before Andre could. Yes, and to apprehend him before the Mounted Police could, to prove to those police that Poleon was—to use their quaint phrasing—a stout fellow, worthy of the job of tracker for the Fort Endurance post.

Almost since Poleon had been old enough to wrap

chubby fingers around a brass button, wide eyes blinking at the scarlet uniform, it had been his unswerving ambition to become a tracker for the Mounted Police.

But they were so blind, these mounties. For their tracker they preferred a big man who, by making faces, could scare babies; one whose talk had the empty bluster of the wind which swept down from the Barren Grounds; one so lacking in woods lore that he could not track a caribou through snow.

That was to say, the police preferred Andre. They were going to make him official tracker for the Fort Endurance post. They were, unless Poleon Baptiste would prove to them what a bold heart beat within his stumpy frame; what firmness, what resolution, what woods-cunning lay behind his mild eyes, his cherubic, smoked-wood face.

In contemplating the changed sign, Poleon remained charitable in his feelings toward the madman. Under the weight of northern solitudes he had known men to break before. Poor shake-brains, they but followed the dictates of phantom voices they alone could understand.

But if the madman had no murder in his heart, he had it in his hands. The unhappy creature had struck first in the Sweetgrass Hills, felling his brother with a broadax. Seventy miles away, on Running Wolf Creek, he had struck again, his rifle dropping an Indian lad who was fishing from his canoe. The madman had stolen the canoe and thereafter his gibbering laughter—and his callous rifle— had sounded on many waterways.

Too inept to hold to the mad killer's trail, Andre had followed Poleon, clinging to him like a shadow through all the Big Thunder land, into the valley of the Okopotowee, and now at last into this muskeg region of interlaced thickets and spider-webbed waterways so remote that half the streams had never been named.

That big one had even lolled in his canoe and made taunting remarks when Poleon, at the portages, drew up and laboriously searched the landwash for signs of the mad killer's passing. In the end, Poleon had been forced to make an "arrangement," sharing his campfire with Andre. *Waugh*, but the arrangement was one of a bitter taste! However, two campfires winking side by side through the night were a great stupidity, surely, doubling the amount of smoke and fire for a warning to the killer.

This morning Andre had not arisen to follow Poleon. That of itself was not strange; the trail was now so hot Andre could follow it alone. The puzzling thing was that now, with every minute counting, Andre had so placidly allowed Poleon to gain this head start.

Mile after mile, he swept along through the clearing mist, and gave himself up to exultation. But as time went on and the canoe of Andre did not appear in sight, a disturbing thought kept crowding in the back of his mind. The thought pushed and swelled, grew finally into a monstrous thing . . . and Poleon drove his canoe ashore on a pea-gravel bar and sat there trembling, his soul sick from a horrible knowledge.

In the first place, there were all the little things of last night at their camp just above the signpost island: Andre's unnatural manner, his curious nervousness, his so-mocking prediction that Poleon would never get the tracking job. But most of all there was the lie he had told about his wet clothes. He had fallen in the water, he said. But when a man falls in water, the water splashes. It does not wet him evenly all around as when he wades. Andre had been evenly wet to the waist—the depth of the water between shore and signpost island.

The absence of canoe marks on the gravelly landwash had troubled Poleon from the first, because had the madman landed on the island he would almost certainly have left them. Yes, the pattern of guilt was clear. Andre's incredible failure to roll from his blanket this morning was incredible no longer. That big one had stayed behind, feigning sleep, expecting Poleon to float to his death down the wrong waterway. It was not the madman, but Andre who had changed the sign . . . There had been always in Andre a streak of ruthlessness. He was a man who, when he could not get what he wanted in one way, got it in another . . . Well, his so-diabolical plan to win for himself the tracking job had failed. Because of this very caution which they called timidity, he, Poleon Baptiste, was still alive. Alive and leading the chase. Andre had defeated himself . . .

Why, Andre had *killed* himself!

But yes! He would come along in his canoe, that careless one. In the mist, he would see little of the river or the shore. He would seek out the sign only, the sign which he himself had made to point the wrong way. And he would let himself be guided by the sign, not knowing that Poleon had changed it back. He would float to eternal darkness in the white waters of the *Rapides du Mort*.

He would . . . unless—

The water boiled as Poleon dug his paddle deep, savagely swerving the canoe. He started paddling—upstream. Half-way back to the water's parting, the police canoes passed him, scudding fast. Those policemen waved a tolerant greeting.

The Sergeant Altward cupped a hand to his mouth and shouted, "What's your hurry going back, Poleon? The loony chasing you?"

Poleon could see the flash of their teeth when they laughed. It was nothing new for them to laugh. He kept paddling.

Poleon found Andre. He found him beside the wreck of his canoe, far down the route to the *Rapides du Mort*. At the last moment, quite obviously, the half-breed had become alarmed at the swiftness of the water, at the deepening of the gorge in which these fierce rapids roared.

He had landed in a panic, running ashore on a shelf of rock which had ripped the whole bottom from his canoe. Now he stood there, as helplessly marooned in this land of interlaced waterways as though he had been wrecked on a South Sea island.

Poleon headed in, made the landing safely. He eyed Andre impassively. "Tak' your paddle an' get in my canoe."

Wheedling words jammed from Andre's lips as he bent in fumbling haste for his paddle. "Togedder, you and me, Poleon, we will get thees mad killer. An' when we have got him I will say to the p'lice: It mak's all the credit to Poleon!"

Poleon stared blankly. "Get in the canoe, liar—liar and sign-changer."

Andre's face turned white as the underside of an aspen leaf. He got in the canoe. Poleon made no threatening move, and then Andre's confidence flowed back as he counseled himself that this stumpy little man was, after all, a rabbit.

Poleon, being lighter, took the forward seat. With a single sweep of his paddle he sent the canoe into the slick of the current—*heading downstream*. Above the roar of those rapids ahead, he heard Andre's voice, ugly with fear. "This way brings death!"

Andre tried desperately to sprag with the flat of his paddle. But they were in the full grip of the current now and there was no perceptible slackening in their speed. Andre half stood up. The canoe wobbled.

Poleon looked around. "Sit down." He grinned thinly. "We will catch the madman togedder, Andre, like you have said."

"You are the madman!" Andre screamed, crouching. "This way you will catch nothing but death for us bot'."

"It mak's ver' possible, yes." Then Poleon explained patiently, as to a child: "If we are to catch the mad killer, this is our single chance. The red-coat p'lice are tracking too, have you forgotten that? If we are to beat them, we have no time to fight the current all the way back to the safe fork. A half day I have wasted already, returning for you. Sit down, Andre—"

"I will not sit down!"

Poleon lifted his paddle from the water, raised it high. Then Poleon, who shrank from clubbing the live mink in his trap, brought the paddle down in a hard, swift blow against Andre's head. The half-breed slumped, unconscious, in the bottom of the canoe.

The canoe rocked . . . but remained afloat. They were in white water now. The canoe dipped and leaped like a bucking horse. But Poleon held it under the mastery of his paddle, gripping the handle so hard that his knuckles appeared as white bumps in the brownness of his hands.

Deep in the gorge now the cliffs reared high, enclosing the noonday sun. The water in its swift flow made white patches as it broke with a sullen roar against fangs of rock.

With eyes slitted against the glare, Poleon crouched and worked as never before in his toilsome life, fighting the white water with a paddle that was bent sometimes almost to breaking as he drove now under the loom of the cliff wall so close that he raked it, now out in the middle, drenched with spray and swerving in the boil of the current to miss outcropping boulders.

Death! So close and so long. Life! So good and so short. Wild geese honking high; the sun on an otter skin; winter air tanged with wood smoke; summer air made crisp and heady from the smell of pines . . . It would be sad to leave all this.

But he need not. Very nearly he had run the whole gantlet of these death rocks, with but one more washboard rapids to be traversed!—

He was in it! Dipping down, tipping . . . he was out of it! So fast, like the blinking of an eye. He had run the *Rapides du Mort* and he floated free! Life—it was in his two hands . . .

No! No, it was not. It was still on the lap of the white water. Because ahead, around this cliff bend, remained the great falls.

Around the bend the canoe sped, the rail sucking water. And at once there was a quickening, a sickening forward lurch, as the craft was gripped from underneath and hurled ahead faster than it yet had gone. Here, as the walls narrowed down, squeezing the sun from the gorge, there was a curious half-hush, more frightful than the water's roar in the upper rapids. It made a pressure against the ears as dead ahead—terrifyingly near—the river poured into the sky.

At the very brink of the falls, two upthrust rocks met the rush of water, forcing it in a swelling mound between them. Poleon made his choice. Between these rocks he would go, as though with the canoe he were threading a giant needle. That much he could accomplish with the deft use of his two strong hands. After that, it was the hands of *le bon Dieu* which must direct.

Below this thunder water was the place where lily pads lay flat on still black pools. No water breaking in white flashes, but only the tranquil loveliness of white lily blooms. Perhaps the lilies would soon become funeral flowers.

It was at the same time a few short seconds and several billion years—then the canoe came pouring with the river into the sky.

He was an eagle soaring.

Then he was tilting down, down, down, in sparkling spume, with the bow of his canoe overshooting the water into the sun. Down and down—a screaming eagle—dropping from the top of the world into tall spruces . . .

Into rocks also. He could see now. Below, through this trough of white foaming hell, were black snags of rock. Ah, but between the rocks there must be water. And the canoe still sailed right-side-up. So why should he die? All those who had come before had died. But that was because the water ran higher or lower in the gorge, or because their canoes had struck rocks, or overturned in the eddies, or—

He was in it. Out of the air and into the water. Into the rocks and the roar. The spray beat overhead as in a solid wave. A whirlpool rapids seized the canoe, spun it—flung it clear to bob among the lily pads in the still black pools below. He could see the lilies. No, funeral flowers they were.

The next instant the waterlogged canoe turned over, as Andre, stirring back to consciousness, thrashed in uncalculated effort. They splashed ashore together, Poleon and the revived Andre, virtually into the arms of the Mounted Police.

There was the whole patrol, the Sergeant Altward and all. For once, those red-coat police were not glib with words. They stood in the willow scrub and stared in frank jaw-dropping wonder.

Against his wet clothes Andre's chest was swelling, and

with the fast returning of his wits he was talking in his accustomed wide way:

"T'rough the rapids an' over the falls we came. Thees wan—" His hand waved out toward Poleon—"He object. But I tell him: these red-coat p'lice are trail the mad killer also. If we are to beat them, we have no time to go by the safe route. We mus' tak' our chance in the *Rapides du Mort* w'ere nevair man before has gone an' lived."

Poleon stumped forward unsteadily on his short legs. "Listen to me w'at I say—" But he was so choked with water and outraged anger that the words caught in his throat.

Andre, who was always so quick with the right words, said, "Don' pay him some attention. He shake han's wit' the willows from w'ere I have to hit him on head wit' my paddle. In great fear, he refuse to run the rapids. I have much trouble wit' him, *oui*. He has delay me greatly."

Poleon ground his teeth. To have earned that tracking job, only to have Andre snatch it from him at this last moment—

But then the hard flat voice of the Sergeant Altward cut through his despair, as the sergeant questioned Andre.

"If Poleon is the coward as you say, and you had to hit him on the head with your paddle, then why is the bump on *your* head instead of Poleon's? Why did we meet Poleon going in the opposite direction on the other branch of the river this morning? Wasn't it because Poleon tossed away his lead in the chase to go back and rescue you when you blundered down the wrong fork of the river? Are you such a clumsy tracker, Andre, that you cannot see a signpost on an island?"

Andre hung his head and said nothing. Poleon couldn't understand at first. But after a moment he did. What *could* Andre say without revealing that he was not only a liar but a sign-changer?

The Sergeant Altward was talking again, looking at Poleon with a sober smile. "The madman's slipped us," he said. "Can you put us back on his trail?"

"By the whiskers of a green musk ox," Poleon sputtered, "I can!"

"You're hired," the sergeant said, "as tracker for the Fort Endurance post."

Poleon swallowed, gasped, drew himself up in the manner of a veritable Bonaparte. "Official?"

"Official," the sergeant assured him.

Fiercely, Poleon frowned. "I accept," he said.

Enough Gold

For SEVEN LONG days and nights the wind had poured out of the Great Canadian Barrens, bending the tall spruces under its blast and piling snow high over the Dolomite Hills. And now the storm had blown itself out. White silence gripped the North.

Halfway up the slope, in a shake cabin several hundred feet above No-name Creek, ore so rich that it revealed more gold than quartz lay shimmering in a high yellow heap on the split-log table.

Big Ed Dekker sat and watched it. He looked bored and unhappy. Once in a while he reached out toward the golden pile and scooped up a handful. Sullenly he would hold it in his hand long enough to get the feel of its solid weight, then drop it back on the tabletop.

But most of the time he sat morosely and stared.

On the other hand his partner, I-like-fish Farrington, looked contented. Or at the very least, philosophically resigned. All it took to please him, apparently, was an empty tin can. He held the can in his hands and turned it around and around. The tough skin of his fingers made a monotonous *shuf-shuffing* sound against the paper wrapper. His lips moved soundlessly.

Suddenly those moving lips formed words out loud.

"Often it serve," he muttered. "Often it serve."

Ed Dekker looked up, startled, from his contemplation of the gold. Seeing his partner's hard-staring eyes, and the lips again making soundless movement, he began to feel goose flesh pricking out on him.

"You gone nuts?" he barked.

I-like-fish, usually shortened to Finny by Ed, who had invented the name in the first place, answered in a dead flat tone. No expression at all to the words, and less sense.

He said: "Often it serve delicious and wholesome packed freshly and waters Alaskan cold in caught is salmon brand iceberg."

"Crazy as a loon!" Ed Dekker said. "Cooped up here all winter, with nothin' to see but white, nothin' to hear but silence, nothin' to eat but salmon out of cans! It's got you shakin' hands with the willows."

"Often it serve," Finny repeated solemnly.

Ed pushed to his feet so fast his stool thumped over backward. "It ain't enough I got to eat canned fish three times a day all winter when I don't like it anyway, but I got to listen to you read the labels all the time tellin' how good it is! And now you can't even read the label straight! I stood enough of your jabber. I stood too much." He came at his partner in a bull rush, long arms flailing.

Finny went down under that unexpected attack. But he didn't stay down. He popped up like a cork in water, swiped the back of his hand across his bloodied nose, and bored in with both fists.

Ed Dekker was a six-footer with a pair of shoulders on him that would have done credit to a mountain grizzly. But I-like-fish Farrington was big, too, and what slight disadvantage he lost in weight he made up in speed.

Toe to toe, they stood and rocked each other with their blows. Hard, bare-knuckled *thups* to the face and chest, and both of them standing into it, not giving an inch.

They had to fight. All the tension pent up through a long winter of getting on each other's nerves seemed to be released in this close-in hammering.

They didn't feel anything at all. The white months,

gnawing their sanity to a thin shrill edge, seemed to have made them impervious to hurt. They might have gone on, absorbing fist jolts until one of them dropped from exhaustion, except that the tipped-over stool got in the way. Ed tripped over it and careened, pulling Finny with him. They hauled up against the table with its high heap of golden ore.

Ed, Finny, the table, and the gold crashed to the floor in a confused jumble.

Sitting in the wreckage of their own making, the partners blinked at each other with dawning comprehension of their folly. They were lifelong friends and here they were fighting. Over nothing.

With a guilty pang Ed recalled the cause of his suddenly aroused fury—Finny's aimless babbling. The white and silent North had caught up with Finny. For a long while it had been a toss-up which of them would crack first. Now Finny had cracked.

A feeling of overwhelming responsibility fell to Ed. Finny would have to be humored, babied even, until a period of association with fellow creatures in less hostile country had set his mind on sane tracks again. And instead of humoring the poor fellow he had started a fight with him!

He sought earnestly to make amends. "Finny, old-timer, I was only funnin' with you."

Finny nodded. "Yeah, I know."

"Salmon's good food," Ed declared. "I like it."

Finny nodded again, "Oven moderate in minutes twenty baked when delicious."

Ed reached out and patted him on the shoulder. "Now you jus' take it easy, Finny old boy."

"You understand what I said?" Finny demanded.

"Sure," Ed said pityingly.

"What did I say?"

Ed scratched at his stubbled jaw. "You said—"

"No use," Finny taunted. "You're too near bushed from sittin' lookin' at the gold every day. You'd never understand me."

"I could try," Ed said tolerantly.

"I was recitin' what the label on the salmon can said."

"That's—what the salmon can said, huh?"

"Sure. Backward."

"Huh?"

"I was memorizin' it backward."

A wild light mounted in Ed's eyes. "You mean you said them words like that on purpose?"

"Nothin' else. Cooped up here all winter with you, that's how I keep from losin' my mind. And if you don't stop broodin' over the gold and get to concentratin' on somethin' like a salmon-can label, you're gonna end up bushed as a dingbat."

"Well, I'm a flat-horned moose!" Ed growled. "Here I thought *you* were bushed, and I'm feelin' sorry for you." His big hand, the same which had patted Finny so sympathetically, doubled into a fist.

Finny dodged the blow and grinned. "We better get our gold swept up," he said.

While they scraped and picked to clear the floor of its golden flood, they talked more amiably than they had in weeks.

"With New Year's long gone a chinook should be blowin' down on us any time now," Finny volunteered. "We wouldn't have to wait for spring. Warm wind out of Oregon would melt enough of this snow in a day so we could maybe take our map and check off enough landmarks to locate the treasure."

"Yeah, if there is any treasure."

"What you mean by that? You were the one that wanted to stay in here this winter. I said we got enough gold, let's get out. You said there's no such thing as enough gold."

"I know. But the more I sit here all winter eatin' salmon and listenin' to you read the labels, the more I think we're a couple dopes to put so much trust in an Indian we never seen till jus' before he died."

"That Chippewyan didn't have any reason to fool us," Finny argued. "We come on him when he was dyin'. We chased off the man that shot him. Then we stayed with him and nursed him right to the end. Indians like to pay back. Only thing he had to give us was the map. I never doubted the map. All I doubted was the wisdom of us casin' up in these wolf-howlin' hills all through a starvation winter when we already had enough gold to make it easy for us on south."

They were filling the last of the pokes with the gold ore when suddenly, amazingly, the door rattled to a hard pounding outside.

"Hallo in there," a muffled voice called.

The two men swapped startled glances.

"Are we both off our nuts?" Finny whispered.

"Nope," Ed said, "we really heard it. I don't quite believe it, that's all. Lookin' at your loose-hung mug all winter, and I was forgettin' there's human bein's left in the world."

"Who'n hell could it be?" wondered Finny.

"We might try openin' the door and findin' out," Ed observed. "Could be a *mètis*, I guess, wanderin' in to tail him out a new fur path."

The door rattled to a renewed banging.

Ed started moving toward the door. "If he's another

label reader I'll jump on his face and make him swallow
a can of salmon whole and unopened!" Looking back, he
whispered hoarsely, "Stow that gold quick, Finny. With
no guns, I wouldn't trust even a missionary."

"You're so danged suspicious," Finny grumbled, "sometimes I wonder if you even trust me."

He kicked the caribou-hide pokes under the bunk and
Ed opened the door.

The man who tumbled inside, spattering snow in all
directions, was a little man. His only observable feature
in that first moment were his eyes. They were peculiar.
They blazed from the depths of his fur dicky hood with
a fixed, unblinking expression like an animal's.

His voice fit those oddly insensitive eyes. It was flat,
impersonal, carrying an animallike purr.

"You fellas are a lifesaver to me," he said, his mouth
cracking into a smile that didn't supply any warmth, but
seemed mechanical almost to the point of inhumanness.

While the stranger peeled out of his bearskin mitts and
parka, the partners stared at him in sober speculation.

"I'm Hymie Fess," the little man volunteered. "Rovin'
free trader."

Out from under the parka and a Hudson's Bay mackinaw he moved toward the sheet-iron stove with the quick-
muscled ease of a squirrel.

"Been lookin' over these creeks," he went on. "Had an
idea I might spot some trappers in here an grubstake
'em." His thin lips twisted, showing glimpses of tiny
pointed teeth. "Ain't enough fur in here to line a vest
pocket! Devil's own country, these Dolomites. I lost my
pack and rifle in a storm, and I ain't et for two days. If
I hadn't run onto you boys—" He sliced his hand in a
suggestive movement across his neck and made a disagreeable clucking noise.

"We lost our own guns when we first come in here late fall," Finny said sympathetically. "If we hadn't landed on this cabin, your bones wouldn't be the only ones stickin' outta the snow next May."

"You mean you got no guns at all?"

It was a natural enough question under the circumstances, but Ed, who had been trying to down an impression of menace ever since Hymie Fess had tumbled inside the door, quit trying to reason it aside, and flashed Finny a quick, warning glance.

But Finny reasoned that if the stranger was going to stay with them any length of time, he'd find out about the guns anyway. And in the meantime Hymie Fess was a welcome break in the monotony of their living. So he ignored Ed's warning.

"No guns," he said. "Don't matter much. Like you said, nothing back in here this season to shoot anyway."

"What have you been livin' on then?" Fess asked.

Ed answered that one. Scowling. "Canned salmon—entire and complete."

Finny pointed to the dark side of the cabin. "Take a look." Hymie Fess left the stove and moved close. His eyes bulged out like peeled grapes when he saw can after can of salmon stacked against the wall.

"Hell! You been livin' like kings."

"Eat nothin' but salmon every day for as long as we have," Ed said sourly, "and you won't call it livin' like kings. You won't even call it livin'."

"I like fish," Finny explained. "But Ed here would take the whole shebang for three beans or a prune."

Hymie Fess couldn't seem to take his eyes away from the salmon. He ran his tongue over his slack lips hungrily. Finny opened a can for him and Fess started wolfing the salmon, sounding a note of animal contentment from somewhere deep in his throat.

"Dry, ain't it?" he said finally, swallowing hard.

"It's some special dry pack, I guess," Finny told him. "So the can'll stand plenty of cold without bustin'."

"How come you to lug 'em all in here?" the little man asked.

"We didn't," Ed said. "We inherited 'em."

"There was a gold-prospectin' party in here last year," Finny explained. "They put up this cabin, such as it is. Someone must have made the feller in charge a deal on a carload of salmon. Anyhow the fish was brought in here to feed a whole crew of men. But the crew never was imported because the vein pinched out. When the prospectin' party went south, salmon bein' too heavy to carry, they left most of it here."

"We heard about it from an Indian," Ed threw in.

"With no gold and no fur in here," Hymie Fess questioned, with his mouth full of salmon, "why the hell did you fellas stay all winter?"

Ed made up a plausible lie. "We got a prospect on farther north," he said. "We want to be all set to jump soon's the snow's off the ground."

"Speakin' of snow off the ground," Hymie Fess grunted, "won't be long, I'm thinkin'. Chinook blowin' down on us. I can feel it in my bones."

Ed and Finny both nodded agreement to that, and Hymie Fess looked up from the table, swiping the back of his hand two ways across his mouth. "Eat some more," Finny urged.

"Enough for now." The little man's predatory glance probed the corners of the cabin. The fingers of one hand drummed on the table top. It was the other hand which caught Ed's eye. He pretended not to see when Hymie Fess thrust his long fingernails in a crack of the table top and pinched out a few tiny flakes of gold.

Ed went over and took his mackinaw down from a peg. "Think I'll step outside for some fresh air. Salmon smell's gettin' too thick for me."

For the next two days the intense cold held, with the wind blowing in blustery gusts from out of the north. Hymie Fess had made himself at home in the cabin. Although there was nothing that could rightly be called suspicious about his actions, even Finny came to feel uneasy in his presence.

The little man, with his oddly fixed eyes, seemed to ooze an attitude of waiting. He seemed strangely like a cat at a game trail. Ed and Finny contrived never to leave him alone in the cabin.

On the morning of the third day they awoke, all three of them, sweltering under their blankets.

"Chinook!" Ed cried.

He bolted out of his bunk and threw the door open wide. Under the drive of a bland southwest wind the snow was melting before his very eyes. From the eaves of the cabin water fell in a steady drip. Inside the cabin, too. The whole floor was puddled from the leaking roof.

"What is this, a cabin or a sieve?" Hymie Fess grumbled.

"Somebody slapped it together pretty fast all right," Finny agreed. "Two-three times this winter we thought the wind would toss us down the gulch in back."

All that day and the next and the next the wind blew warm and strong. The sun shone, too, and between the unseasonable wind and the sun, the snow continued to vanish as though by magic. Patches of bare black rock appeared on the slope below the cabin. Above it a nest of dolomite boulders poked through. Big fellows. Big as a cabin, some of them.

Both Ed and Finny had memorized the map which pointed the way to the burial place of Chippewyan treasure. They did the best they could to conceal from Hymie Fess their avid interest in the melting away of the snow blanket which all winter had concealed the landmarks indicated on the map.

By now some of these landmarks were unmistakably revealed. The partners conferred nervously with each other whenever they could get a few minutes out from under the patiently watchful eyes of Hymie Fess. They trusted Hymie less than ever now. On the first morning of the chinook he had produced a revolver from a concealed shoulder holster and had spent the greater part of the day polishing it and testing its action.

"Thought you'd lost your guns," Ed said.

"All but this one." Hymie's voice was an animallike purr.

All in all, Hymie Fess was fast becoming the partners' number-one problem. How they were going to go about tracking down the treasure with the sly little man eternally watching them was worrying Ed and Finny more than they wanted to admit.

Hymie didn't help their ease of mind by something he said one day. Gazing out at the new contours uncovered in the rugged Dolomite Hills by the melting snow, he remarked unemotionally, "If anyone had a map and they were waitin' for the snow to go, so's to check off landmarks, now'd be the time, wouldn't it?"

Just before dark on the third day of the warm winds something happened to divert the partners' minds from their growing worry. Water was trickling in tiny rivulets everywhere and suddenly, from a little way up the steep slope, a bank of snow let go. It *swooshed* past the cabin in a sinuous flow, a miniature avalanche, down, on down four hundred feet until it disappeared over a precipice into the gorge below.

In passing, it loosened the cribbed slide rock which had been thrown up as a foundation for the cabin. The cabin developed a pronounced sag, and Ed, Finny, and Hymie Fess, all three, worked like beavers until long after dark bolstering the shaky structure.

Then they each ate a can of salmon—Hymie Fess with evident relish, Finny with resignation, Ed with blasphemous mutterings and facial contortions registering acute displeasure—and piled into their blankets.

The last thing Ed said before he went to sleep was, "I can't choke down another bite—Never. I wisht an avalanche would cart away every last can of salmon we got in the place."

None of them slept well that night. The temperature stayed above freezing and hour after black hour water everywhere dripped and gurgled. Several times the slurring roar of a snowslide echoed from nearby hills.

The gray smudge of dawn was in the sky when Ed and Hymie Fess were awakened, and Finny was thrown clear of his bunk by a crashing jolt which shook the whole cabin.

"Some of them dolomite boulders up above has let go!" Finny diagnosed the case.

The three men crowded for the door in the bare nick of time. Another splintering crash slewed the cabin three feet around on its slide rock base, and precipitated the partners and Hymie Fess out of the door on their faces.

They scrambled to their feet with the sound of that splintering still loud in their ears. Down the slope, echoing away from them, they could hear the pounding thud of the unseated boulder which had slewed the cabin around as it made its way to the oblivion of the gorge below.

No more rocks came tumbling, and Finny stuck his head inside the door. He looked out again quickly. There was enough light in the morning sky to show his face, gray and shaken.

"You've got your wish, Ed," was all he said.

"Huh? How you mean?"

"Take a look for yourself. That last chunk of rock knocked the whole side of the cabin out. Every last can of salmon is avalanched clear to the bottom of the gorge. The gold, too, that was under the bunk."

Working frantically, they cleared the cabin of their remaining gear, then waited miserably for the sun to poke its first red fingers between the high hills. In the full light of the day Ed examined the gaping hole in the side of the tilted cabin and did some emergency shoring while Finny scoured the slope for some sign of a salmon can or a glint of the golden ore.

Finny didn't find anything. The sliding snow and rock had swept clean, carrying everything down and dumping it into the inaccessible gorge below. He dragged wearily back to the cabin and Ed read the answer in his dull eyes.

Neither of them said anything, but both realized they were so close to death that it was all over but the dying. The chinook would blow itself out and winter would clamp down again. It would be six weeks at least before they could get out of these starvation Dolomite Hills. Six weeks. And all they had to eat was a handful of tea leaves which Ed had garnered leaf by leaf from the cabin wreckage. They'd be lucky to last six days.

"Anyhow it'll be a relief not to have to eat no more salmon," Ed said, with a faint grin.

In the tragic awareness of their greater loss neither of

them gave any thought to the gold. Nor to Hymie Fess. All morning the hardeyed little man had sat on a rock and watched silently, offering no help.

Now suddenly his rasping voice jerked Ed and Finny to realization of other things besides the loss of their food.

"Look around, you two dimwits!"

The same thought leaped to both of them. On the slope above, from where the dolomite boulder had rolled down to wreck the cabin, there was another huge boulder perilously balanced. Hymie Fess, they thought, must be sounding a warning about it.

They looked around, and there was the boulder the same as ever. And there was Hymie Fess with no more expression on his face than it had ever showed. But he was covering them with his revolver.

"I want the map," he said tersely.

"What map?" asked Finny.

"The only map there is. The one you got off the Chippewyan."

"What're you talkin' about?" Finny asked dully.

"Don't stall," Hymie Fess snarled. "It was dark. You didn't see me so good, I guess. But I saw you. I snuck back after you'd took my guns and chased me off. I watched you in the light of your campfire. I wasn't outfitted to hang close on your trail. It took me a while. But I found you." The revolver moved threateningly. "Hand over that map!"

"So you were the one!" Ed growled. "I thought there was somethin' about you—you were the one who was torturin' the Chip—"

Hymie Fess growled like an animal ready to spring. "The map!"

"Here it is." Finny reached inside his clothes, pulled out a folded piece of thin caribou hide. He tossed it, and

Hymie Fess caught and unfolded the native-cured parchment with one hand.

Out of the tail of his eyes he examined it and grunted in quick satisfaction.

"I'll let you live till I check on this," he told the two partners. "Hadn't ought to take long. Looks like the Indian's buried his treasure close."

"Won't do you no more good'n it's doin' us," Finny said, in apathetic warning.

"Oh, yeah? Why won't it?"

"Because there's nothin' to eat. You'll never get out of the Dolomites without food."

"Looks like I'm way ahead of you on that," Hymie Fess said softly.

Finny frowned. "How d'you mean?"

The little man chuckled malevolently. "If it comes to that, there's always you two."

Ed was nodding quietly. He knew it about this little man from the first, he was telling himself. Hymie Fess was the kind eminently fitted to survive in this country. No more feelings, no more sensitivity than a hungry animal.

Hymie Fess put it into words. "I been noticin' you close. I estimate you two would dress down to a couple hundred pounds, easy, of nourishin' meat."

They watched him as he backed away with the revolver. At a little distance he turned and strode along, cocky as a wolverine that has buried a fat carcass in anticipation of another day's hunger. They watched him stoop to grab up one of their own miner's picks, then disappear around a snow-pillowed shoulder of gray granite.

Alone, they stared at each other.

"We could follow him," Finny suggested doubtfully.

"Maybe it'd be better to wait for him here," Ed rumbled.

"He might not come back," Finny said thoughtfully. "If it's like he said, that he's been on our trail instead of just stumbling in here accidentally while lookin' over the creeks for fur, then he's probably got a cache of food somewhere near. I remember thinkin' that first day he showed in that he didn't eat much salmon for a starvin' man."

"I caught that, too," Ed told him. "That's why I went outside to look at his tracks before the wind buried 'em. I found his pack and I took it and hid it."

Finny's voice kindled with new interest. "And you never said nothin' about it to me?"

"You know how it's been between us, cooped up here all winter. We ain't either one been givin' the other credit for a lick of horse sense. With Hymie Fess not showin' actually hostile, I was afraid you'd think I was bushed as a loon for being so suspicious of him. You been crabbin' all your life I'm too suspicious. So I thought I'd wait a little while and see how he turned out. But he was waitin', too. And now it's too late for anything, looks like."

"Maybe not," Finny said with growing excitement. "There's a pack, you said. With food—"

"There was a pack," Ed corrected dismally. "When the chinook came, the pack got washed out from where I hid it. It's playin' tag now down in the gulch with our salmon."

"All right," said Finny, accepting the inevitable, "it's gone. We'll have to think of somethin' else. But when Hymie Fess misses it he'll come back here—"

"To kill us and eat us!"

"Yeah." Finny rubbed his gloved hand against his stubbled jaw. There was a speculative look in his eyes.

"You thinkin' about the same thing I am?" growled Ed.

"Guess so," Finny said slowly. "I'm wonderin' how hungry we'd have to get before it would be a pleasure to bite into Hymie Fess."

"It'd be about as appetizin' a meal as some barbwire dipped in rattlesnake poison," Ed declared. "I'd sooner even eat salmon."

"Well, whether we eat him or not," Finny said practically, "we can't just squat here and leave him eat us."

Ed's bleak glance was ranging upward in the direction of the dolomite boulders uncovered by the melting snow. When the big one which had wrecked the cabin had let go, it had sheered a slice of the gravel slope off with it, creating a stable level except for the solitary boulder which half overhung the scalped slope near the top.

Finny was noticing where Ed's glance held. His eyes glinted. "I think we got somethin' there," he breathed.

Ed swore softly in that breathless way a man does when he's got the answer to something so pat that he won't quite let himself believe it.

"Maybe I'm a shade quicker'n you," Finny observed. "I better work down here and you take the top."

"All the danger's down here," Ed grumbled. "I might start an avalanche that would bury you both."

"I think most of the loose stuff's already gone down. The boulder is all. I'll be watchin' close. I can duck it."

"What if he ducks it, too? He's quick as lightnin'."

"Leave him duck. All I'll be lookin' for is to shift his attention long enough to grab his gun."

"You be careful," Ed warned, gruff concern in his voice.

"Sure."

"I mean careful."

"Sure."

When Hymie Fess came back, Finny was bent over pretending to be doing something with rocks. If Hymie Fess wanted to have good footing when he braced Finny with the revolver there was only one place for him to stand. Everywhere else around, the partners had piled snow or pried rocks on edge.

So Fess stood where they wanted him to, with his back to the slope and on a dead line with the boulder. Finny heard him, of course, but he pretended not to. He didn't look up until Hymie Fess started to curse him.

Then Finny straightened as though in surprise. "Why, what's the matter, Hymie? Seems like a man that had just annexed a treasure would be a mite happy and pleased about it."

Hymie was standing a few feet away, his revolver leveled and all, his wiry body—with the exception, strangely enough, of the hand which held the gun—quivering in rage. His face grimaced, the thin lips working over the pointed teeth.

Finny looked at him in amazement that was not at all feigned. "Didn't you find the treasure, Hymie?"

"I found it," the little man snarled.

"Wasn't there enough gold to suit you? Or what?"

"There wasn't any gold! And if you don't do some tall talkin' before I count to three, I'll feed a slug through your wide mouth just as a warnin' to your partner that Hymie Fess don't stand for monkeyshines. I'm countin'. One . . . two—"

Finny took his cap off and scratched at his head. Ed, watching anxiously for this signal, popped into view from his rocky covert above and gave the boulder a push.

"Look out behind you!" Finny bellowed as Hymie Fess's mouth was pursed to say "three."

Hymie Fess could plainly hear the crashing slam of the

boulder as it bounced downward, so he knew Finny's warning wasn't faked.

He blazed a single shot, but his body was jerking when he pulled the trigger, and so was Finny's. So the first shot did no good—or no harm, according to the point of view.

The boulder which Ed had unloosened was as big as a table, and the clattering crash it made sounded louder by the split second. There was no getting away from it; Hymie Fess had to risk a look upward to see which way to jump. That was where Finny had it on him. Finny had been in position to see how the boulder was rolling from the start. He knew before Fess knew it, which way the little man would jump.

Consequently he was there a wink ahead of Hymie.

The breath was half knocked out of the venomous little man as he collided with Finny. He must have thought the boulder had caught up with him after all, because he screamed like any stricken animal. At the same time he blazed another shot from his gun.

The bullet and the boulder slammed past in the same breath, and Hymie Fess tipped over backward with Finny riding him down. Finny's solid weight was too much for Hymie, and this time the other half of his breath was knocked out of him. Finny landed a right and a left to the jaw to make sure Hymie stayed out for a while. Then, prying the revolver from Hymie's nerveless fingers, he stood up, roaring in triumph to Ed, who was clumping down the slope, leaving a young avalanche in the wake of his seven-league strides.

"Nice goin'," Ed shouted, puffing. "Nice goin', Finny."

Finny shook his head, sobering down. "Somethin's way wrong. Hymie Fess found where the treasure was supposed to be. That Chippewyan must have been havin' a pipe dream. No gold there, Hymie claimed."

Ed stared lugubriously. "Hell, and after us stayin' up here all winter eatin' canned salmon—Hey, wait a minute!" Sudden joy lighted his face. "Somethin' I forgot to tell you. Look."

A few long strides carried him to their tin-can dump just outside the cabin. His gloved hands dived into the pile, and after a few minutes' searching he brought up a can from underneath, brushed off the snow, hurried back to Finny, and put the can in his hands.

The can plummeted from Finny's hands before he could look at it. It simply bored through his loosened grasp, like a lead weight falling, and sank into the snow.

Finny picked it up and pulled open the loose jagged lid. The bright sun played on the contents, bringing out soft yellow glints.

"Gold ore!" Finny gasped.

Ed was watching him, grinning. "Sure."

"Where in blazes did it come from?"

"It's ours. The same we been hoardin' all winter. Hidin' Hymie Fess's pack wasn't the only thing I done. I took our gold from under the bunk and put it in the tin cans for safe keepin'. I figured if it came to a showdown, old tin cans out in plain sight would be the last place Fess would think to look for gold."

"Then . . . then last night when the rock hit, our gold never went down the gulch with the salmon!"

"Nope. It's every bit in these cans."

"Looks like you mighta told a fella somethin' about it," Finny said a little resentfully.

Ed shrugged. "What's the use? With our food gone, it didn't seem very important." The animation drained out of his face. "Hell, it ain't important now, is it? For a minute I was forgettin'."

"Me, too," said Finny glumly.

"Gold or no gold, without food we're—"

"Goners."

The wind was beginning to change, they both noticed. It was a cold wind, a foretaste of the gale that soon would be hurling fresh snow out of the north to smother all trace of the chinook's bland warmth.

Hymie Fess had been moaning. Now he sat up unsteadily.

Ed looked balefully at the little man. "I don't think I could ever do it," he told Finny, shaking his head hopelessly. "I believe I'd sooner eat more salmon."

"Salmon," Hymie Fess moaned. "Salmon—might be treasure to a Chippewyan—but it's only canned fish to me."

The partners both jumped at him. They slapped and shook him back to full consciousness. "What's that you're sayin'?" Ed demanded.

"I thought it was gold," Hymie Fess blubbered. "The Chip admitted he swiped a treasure from the prospectin' party in here and cached it in a cave. I made him draw me a map. Naturally I thought he meant gold. I just now found the cave. *And it's full of salmon. Nothin' but salmon!*"

A look of philosophical calm passed over I-like-fish Farrington's face.

Ed Dekker seemed stunned. "Salmon the on bring," he croaked weakly. "Often it serve—often it serve!"

Giant Killer

The ONLY SAFE place in a coal mine, they said, was out of it—and so every miner had a brass check with his number on it. When all the numbers were dropped in Jojo Kwiatkowski's box at the end of a shift it meant that everybody was up on top, safe for another day anyway.

Before Jojo had cut the sides down and tacked on the leather carrying strap, the box had held dynamite. Now it held life. That was how he liked to think about it.

The lift carried three tons of coal or twelve men. It was Jojo's job to stand all day at the bottom of the Morning Glory shaft and pull the rope that rang the bell that let the hoisting engineer know when to make the cage go up. It was a sad and incomprehensible thing, but some of the miners with whom he shared the underground dangers did not appreciate the importance of his job.

Some of them, dropping their life-checks in his box before they stepped on the cage to go up, made faces at him and barked like a dog.

Killer Sobczyk was the worst—Sobczyk, who was not a killer with a knife or the gun but was called Killer only because it was so easy for him to have his way with another man's woman.

It had all started at the carnival which came every year to the mule pasture by the railroad, bringing naked women dancing in a tent, beautiful presents to be won from clicking wheels, and things to ride on going around fast while girls laughed, holding to their skirts, and boys laughed, holding to the girls. The carnival was one of the wonderful things about America; but this year big pictures had bent in the wind, advertising strange creatures which never should be.

Inside the tent after you paid your money the creatures were not so much. There had been one: half dog, half boy, so the man with the hoarse voice said. Jojo Kwiatkowski had walked slowly around it, observing it carefully. It was a cheat, not real. But Killer Sobczyk had shouted so all could hear, "Thees Dog-face boy, he has your name. Jojo! He looks lak you."

It was not true. Jojo would admit that his legs were a little short, his face maybe a little ugly. But not *that* short; not *that* ugly. This he had attempted reasonably to explain. But, to his shame, "Jojo, Dog-face Boy," they called him still.

After today they would not.

It was a vow he had made last night in the saloon— early, when he was still sober. His good friend of the Old Country, Casimir Unanski, had witnessed—Casimir who had sly, sullen-mouthed Luba for a wife, and who should have been making a vow of his own.

Now that the time was so near, Jojo could feel his skin crawl, steamy-hot, under his pit clothes. He could look down the line of coal-blackened miners awaiting their turn to go up on the cage, and he could see Killer Sobczyk there, his shoulders bulking like a crib of timbers, his flat eyes in his flat face staring.

Almost time for him to start the not-funny joking, dropping his life-check so that it fell outside the box, knowing that Jojo, the keeper of the checks, must stoop to pick it up. That was when the Killer would run in, barking and calling Dog-face Boy, and stamping with his heavy pit shoes—and everybody laughing to see Jojo on his stumpy legs, jerking away so fast that sometimes he fell over backward.

Yesterday he had not jerked away fast enough. That was why today the fingers of one hand had bandages. Maybe the Killer had not meant actually to step on them, but he had anyhow laughed to see Jojo jumping around shaking his hurt fingers.

He would not laugh any more.

Closer and closer now the Killer was moving up with the line. He would be with the next bunch to step on the cage.

Jojo had planned well. Last night he had practiced, taking the pillow from his bed and putting it against the back of a chair, running then from across the room and throwing himself full strength—well, almost full strength—and butting the pillow with his head.

He made so much noise that men who had come back early from the saloons and were trying to sleep swore at him from out of the boardinghouse windows.

He had been ready to quit anyway. Feathers puffing from the pillow floated in the room like snow. The chair was broken, his head ached some and his neck was sore. But he had learned how to treat Killer Sobczyk the next time he ran in barking and stamping. After the butting there might remain some small cleanup work with fists— or a chunk of coal. Then neither Sobczyk nor any of them would laugh at him again, or bark, or call Dog-face Boy.

His good friend, Casimir, had been much troubled to hear his intent.

"You watch out, Jojo," he warned. "Thees Sobczyk, I know him well. He is lak animal. He cares nothing for anything but only himself. He is big and he is mean and he cares nothing."

Waugh—but that was a timid man talking! A thin man with no hair in front, bent in the shoulders from too much shoveling of coal under a low top, and with a mustache that drooped like a dog's tail—a man who worked also a mile inside the dark mine where it would be easy for anyone to get behind him and make an "accident"—a man who had also a wife pleasing to lady-killer Sobczyk. Casimir had reasons to be afraid.

With Jojo it was different. He was bold. He was strong. He had no wife. And here under the electric light where he stood all day and made the cage go up and down, no one could creep up behind him.

While he was about it, he made a vow for Casimir too. It was like what they said, two birds with one rock. In defending his own good name he could at the same time fight for Casimir's. Yes, when a man had a friend so close, like Casimir, his own great shame must be your shame, his dishonor your dishonor. This remained true even though Casimir in his gentle way had told him to mind his own business.

"You leave to me thees Sobczyk, Jojo. When it is time, I do something, you bet."

Jojo had pressed the arm of his friend in a strong and understanding way, and repeated his vow, though silently, that never any more would they laugh behind the back of Casimir because of his cheating wife.

Clanking at the end of its cable, another man-cage dropped though the roof, settling with a jar at the landing. The men at the head of the line crowded forward, and Killer Sobczyk was one of them. So now was the time—right now. Jojo was ready, with his legs braced and his shoulders bent. There was only one thing wrong. Casimir had promised to be close in the line to watch. He was not here and that was curious. He was not here—and suddenly Jojo was glad.

In a moment of self-damnation which seared him, he told himself they were right to call him Dog-face Boy. He deserved nothing better, because with the Killer's flat eyes mocking and his hand swinging down to drop the life-check, Jojo knew he was going to scratch dirt, as always, and pick up the life-check and put it in the box and scuttle back from those stamping-pit shoes like a squeaking mouse.

Something almost unbelievable happened then. While Jojo stared in black misery the Killer's hand completed its swing, reaching all the way down to the box. It seemed to cover the whole space inside the box, and to Jojo's ears came the soft metallic splash of the Killer's brass check as it dropped among the others.

The Killer straightened. "A-llo, Jojo."

He took his place with the other miners on the cage. No stamping, no barking, no Dog-face Boy!

Jojo felt his teeth chattering, and that was the first he knew that his cold cigar had dropped from his mouth. The Killer had not joked him. Why? Rattling between the wooden guide rails, the cage swooped up and down in the dark shaft, and after a while Jojo quit trying to think why. Sometimes it was best to take the good things as they came, not examining too closely. His moment of weakness and shame was known only to himself. He could explain to Casimir that there had been no need to butt the Killer because, sensing the firm resolve, the Killer had already started to treat him with respect.

Eagerly then, Jojo kept watching to catch the first glimpse of his friend. But the line shortened, dribbled out to a few stragglers . . . Jojo always went up on the last cage with the bosses.

"Get your bucket and come on," one of them told him.

"No," Jojo said, "Casimir—he don' come out yet. Is still in coal mine."

"You're crazy. I just came from the check board. It's clean."

"How can be? You hold cage, hah? I go see."

In the near manway Jojo stared at the big board with the numbers on it. Empty, like the boss said. No checks on the board meant that they were all in Jojo's box, and that every man of the day shift was out of the mine. He stared hard at 241, Casimir's number. It seemed that if he looked hard enough the check must appear on the nail. Because how could his friend go up and Jojo, guardian of the cage, not know?

The foreman had an answer.

"Casimir must have loaded his four cars early and walked up the air shaft. You were around bumming a match for your cigar when he came by and pitched his check in your box."

Jojo shrugged. It must be true. And yet how could Casimir have forgotten his promise to be close in the going-up line to watch the butting of Killer Sobczyk? There was much talk to make with Casimir, yes.

Above ground Jojo snorted around under the shower at the washhouse and changed into his top clothes. He started walking to the boardinghouse with his two-deck aluminum bucket wedged between hip and elbow, eyes slitted against the late summer sun, nose titillated by the musky-sweet smell of tasseling corn blown in from fields hemming the town.

Nearing the railroad crossing he hurried and climbed

on the train that was pulling out with the day's coal flats. He hung by one hand to a dusty grab iron and had a free ride for the rest of the way.

After supper he walked downtown to Warsaw Willie's saloon, puffing a fresh cigar. It was the biggest ten-cent cigar he could buy. Jojo liked big things: heaped dinner plates, thick mugs of beer, big women, fat cigars that filled his face.

In the saloon he looked around for Casimir. Every night they met here for drinks, for card games, for good talk about the day's work. Also good talk about women—in the saloon, away from women, away from Casimir's cheating wife.

So crazy how it was about Casimir's woman. A man had only to take a bus to Carbon River where a hundred women waited, each more better than Luba. But would Casimir go with him even once to find out? No. The most he would do was boast sometimes that one day his wife and everybody would see him no more. He would come up from the mine and climb on the coal train and go away and never come back. This, as everyone knew, was only whisky-bragging.

Warsaw Willie, bulking pink and moist behind his bar, saw Jojo looking around and he called out, "Not here yet."

Jojo kept looking anyway, with dignity, ignoring the barks and Dog-face calls that came as he peered into each of the wooden booths. In back there was a gambling room. Oilcloth covered the windows. The green-shaded bulb hanging low over the poker table was not yet lighted. Jojo snapped it on.

Casimir wasn't here. But someone else was. Killer Sobczyk.

The light coned down on his bottle of whisky, and on

his big hand squashed against the round table top, cuddling the shot glass.

The Killer swore when the light pierced his eyes—slate-blue eyes that turned a muddy yellow color with his drinking. "Get out!"

Jojo got out. He pushed his way to the rail at the noisy bar and had two whiskies fast. Killer Sobczyk in there drinking—When a man sat alone and got drunk this early it was because he wanted to forget something. Or because he was afraid of something.

What would the Killer be afraid of?

Jojo knew the answer, but it was so tremendous that he tantalized himself by pretending that he didn't. He drank two more whiskies. Slow. Then he bought a fresh cigar, a fifteen-cent one, and let Warsaw Willie light it for him. He watched himself scowl in the bar mirror, then swung away, trailing smoke, heading toward that back room where Killer Sobczyk sat alone. Drinking because he was afraid.

Afraid of Jojo Kwiatkowski!

In the coal mine Jojo had not let himself believe it. But now—The Killer was, after all, a bully; he joked only timid men. Yesterday he had stamped on Jojo's fingers, and Jojo had shouted loud threats after him. The cage had not been going up so very fast when he shouted. And today he had stood ready to butt the Killer—for a little while he had—and this the Killer must have sensed.

At the doorway to the back room Jojo pulled the cigar from his mouth and blurted: "Today some life-check. You put she in the box—"

He stopped right there because in his stomach he felt a great and sudden emptiness. He had meant to finish boldly: "You better make damn' sure you put she in the box every damn' day like today—or be more worse for you, Killer—lady-killer only. Also no more Dog-face Boy—and no more to monkey with the woman of Casimir."

All this he had meant to say. But with anger smearing so fast over the Killer's flat face, Jojo had felt his tongue grow thick in his mouth.

It was Killer Sobczyk who broke the tension. Not with violence. Softness!

"My friend, Jojo. Siddown. Have some drink."

The big hand pushed the bottle close on the dirt-glazed cloth and a wheedling look replaced the fierceness in the eyes.

Jojo popped the cigar in his mouth and puffed furiously, making a smoke screen to hide behind while weighing this supreme gesture of conciliation. Something was very, very much not right. The Killer should be *some* afraid of him. But not this much!

He turned away as he left the back room, his shoulder struck the doorjamb, and he walked quickly down the long smoky room toward the street door. This was not a one-man job, no. It was a matter for urgent discussion with Casimir.

He looked through every saloon in town. He did not find Casimir. Through dark streets, then, smelling of crushed cinders and old road tar, he walked toward his friend's house. It must be—it had to be—that tonight Casimir had stayed home with his wife.

It was too much to hope that he had taken Jojo's advice about her. Tough was the way to be with women like Luba. Jojo knew women. Didn't he go every Saturday night to Carbon City where his money was as good as any man's? Jojo knew a hundred women and Casimir but one. But never would his friend take advice about her.

He even tried to *give* advice.

"What you need, Jojo, I tell you, is woman for make nice home with you away from boardinghouse."

That was all right for Casimir to say. Even he did not understand completely how it was for a man they called Dog-face Boy. Very hard for such a one to find a woman who would love from the heart. Something he would admit to no man—or woman—but in the mine and out of it, in his blood and his breathing, the hopeless wish was there.

At Casimir's house the door was opened quickly to his knock. It was Luba who peered from the doorway. The light behind her came from a lamp that grew out of an elephant's back, and had orange ruffles on the shade. Jojo had won it at the carnival and he gave it to Casimir as a present.

He had to admit that the lamp put a nice brightness in Luba's hair. It was shiny on her shoulders too, and on her hips where the green dress was tight and silky.

Jojo, a reasonable man, would concede that this woman might be pleasing to some. But only to a man of inexperience, like Casimir. Or to one of no discrimination, like Killer Sobczyk. Long legs, high breasts—there was not enough meat on her anywhere.

"So—it is you," she said.

Jojo answered stiffly, "Please to tell Casimir—"

"Casimir," she interrupted in her shrill and always complaining voice, "is not here."

Jojo took the cigar from his mouth. "Casimir is not here?" he repeated slowly.

"He did not come home from the mine. It is the first time—" She bit her lip. "Go look in the saloons."

Jojo stared so long that she stirred uneasily and the shiny dress rustled softly. "What is the matter?" Luba asked.

"I have look already."

She gave a nervous shrug. "Then for some overtime work he has stayed in the mine."

"Does a man stay in the mine and his life-check come out?" Jojo's hand feeding the cigar to his face in small, quick stabs, trembled. He went on carefully, so carefully: "The boss say Casimir has come up air shaft."

"You talk not like yourself," she scolded. "Why would Casimir climb so many steps when there is the cage to ride on?"

"Is dark on the steps," Jojo reminded her cryptically. "No one could see him. He could come up and climb on freight train that takes away the coal flats. Suppose if Casimir has ride away with the coal? Other men have done this—"

"But why—"

"Maybe to leave his wife for new woman."

Jojo grinned wickedly, and he could hear her breath catch.

"But Casimir never would!"

"All ri', call me liar. Call me some more liar about Killer Sobczyk."

She leaned close, her mouth thin. "What about him?"

"Gone too," Jojo lied grandly. "Bot' men tired of cheating woman. You make them burn too long inside. Now they make you burn. They leave you, bot' Killer and Casimir."

She stood glaring, and Jojo sensed with satisfaction her gathering fury. Soon enough she would find that he had lied about the Killer. But for a little space let her feel not wanted, as poor Casimir had been for so long not wanted.

With awkward energy he reached out and pushed her backward through the doorway. "Go lay on bed and kick and cry some."

He pulled the door shut so hard the glass rattled. Tough was the way to be with women like Luba.

But outside the gate of Casimir's yard Jojo was not tough any more. He sat down on the edge of the dusty cement sidewalk with his feet in the weeds of the ditch. He sat down in the darkness and now he did not hold back how he felt. He hugged himself and rocked back and forth and cried with shaking sobs.

He had lied to Luba about more than Killer Sobczyk. Lies? They were all lies. In Carbon River lived a hundred women more better than Luba. But Casimir would never leave her, and Jojo knew this well.

Something else he knew well. A dog-face fool he had been to think that Killer Sobczyk was afraid of him. The Killer's so-strange action today in the mine, putting the life-check correctly in the box—It was easy to understand now. In the saloon too—the killer drinking himself drunk, not because he was afraid of something, *but to forget something.*

There was one more place to look for Casimir. Jojo got up and dragged himself to the mine yard, stopping first at the boardinghouse to get his lamp and a flask of carbide. At the brick building which housed the steam-driven fan—that great tireless lung of the coal mine—his hands felt around until they found a rusty iron ring attached to a steel door . . . At the top of the air shaft he could feel the cool blackness that lay under the earth reach up for him, and he could hear the coal mine's hurricane breathing. He put the lamp in his cap and started down the iron grille steps.

Four hundred and twenty-six feet below the streets of the town he came out on the bottom and turned into the

Main South air course, leaning backward, almost sitting down on the wind that rushed him along. His light flowed ahead in the air tunnel, soaking up the blackness in front, letting it press in again from behind.

When he was about a mile inside, he put his shoulder against a wooden ventilating door and stepped out of the wind into a stub entry. Here the air was hot, thick, dead, and heavy with the smell of coal. Distantly on a haulage entry he could hear the rumble of a night-shift track motor.

Moving again, he came soon to the 16th East entry, and he followed the track into Casimir's working room. Ahead, on past the first and second crosscuts, his light picked up the squat bulks of pit cars. He kept on until he had squeezed past their splintery-oak sides and stopped at the working face. Here the coal, blown from the wall by black-powder cartridges the size of a man's arm, lay tumbled in a shiny heap, ready for tomorrow's loading.

He thought where he would go if he wanted to cover up anything so no one would stumble over it—then he turned back and went into the second crosscut off the left rib wall. He poked around, and found Casimir's body there.

It was gobbed over with a thin covering of slate and rock. Blood matted into the hair at the back of the head told what had happened. Jojo stood for so long, bent and staring, that the flame in his lamp grew short and the coal mine shadows crept close.

With a coldness on his heart he reviewed his dark knowledge. Casimir had, after all, made a vow of his own. It must be so. He had told Killer Sobczyk to keep away from his woman. The way, exactly, it had happened then— whether in quick anger, a fight, or whether the Killer had come up from behind in the dark—either way, Casimir had had no chance.

Jojo's hand moved numbly, unfastening his lamp from its clip on his pit cap. He turned the flame overhead. There was loose top in this crosscut. The Killer could have brought the roof down to cover his crime more deeply. Most possibly there had not been time. He had needed to go out and lift Casimir's life-check from the board.

Easy to understand it all now. When the Killer had put his own life-check so properly in the box, he had put in Casimir's also, hiding what he did with his big hand— not making barks and calling Dog-face Boy because, having just killed a man, he wanted to attract no attention to himself.

Jojo's hand moved suddenly to cover the reflector in his lamp and smother the flame. The blackness of the mine swaddled him, and he pushed against it, moving a few steps to the mouth of the crosscut. He waited, hearing only the soft, interminable pressure-crackle of the coal. But a moment before, his ears, sharp from a lifetime of underearth listening, had detected something else. It could be rats. Or it could be Killer Sobczyk coming back in here to finish his job.

From near the room-neck a lamp sparked on. The reflector behind it spread the light between the coal walls. It picked out Jojo. Behind the lamp glare he could not see. But he could hear. The sound was Killer Sobczyk laughing. Drunk-laughing. But not too drunk, or he could not have walked down all those wet and slippery stairs in the air shaft.

Jojo could feel his scalp grow tight where his hair tugged under his pit cap. The hateful tightness spread down and across his chest so that he could not breathe.

It knotted his stomach. It bound his running muscles, while the light bobbed closer and the scuff of shoes on track ties came louder. And then the Killer was standing with his legs spread wide like tree trunks bracing the body, the mouth pushing out slow words.

"Now I bury two instead of one. I mak' nice deep grave to last one million year. They not look for Casimir in coal mine because his life-check say he go up. They not look for you, Jojo; yours never say you come down. Dose life-checks cannot lie, no? All ri, my friend Jojo, Dog-face Boy—"

The last ounce of strength seeped from Jojo's body with the sweat that prickled, hot, everywhere under his clothes. He could see the Killer moving in, the big hands outreaching, the shoulders hunched.

It could have been a memory of Casimir, listening and nodding, his face sometimes gently chiding, but never laughing while Jojo made the big empty talk—Life burst now inside of Jojo like dynamite blasting. It loosened his running muscles. Now he could get away, lose himself in the dark clutter of space hollowed from the coal.

But he didn't run away. He went forward instead, as he had practiced it with the chair and pillow. Full strength this time, like a billy goat butting.

So hard his head squashed into the wide belly that he felt the jolt go through his neck and quiver down his backbone. There was a whiplike motion to the Killer's backward fall, so that the top part of his giant body hit much harder than the middle.

That was all there was to it. His head lolled where it had struck against the rail, the lamp awry in its pit-cap clip but still flaming. The blood showed black in the light, but the Killer's face, Jojo could see, had already some of the whiteness of death. No need to pick up a piece of slate; the steel rail had done the job.

Jojo's hands moved in an empty swing at his side. He felt tired, as after a hard day's work well done—

Not quite done.

Bending, he dragged Killer Sobczyk's dead body near Casimir's. Then he went and got a pick from Casimir's toolbox. He came back and loosened the cap pieces and took down the oak crossbars that held up a loose section of top. Then with the pick he attacked the ledge, working skillfully as any miner knows how, to bring the bad top down. He worked fast because there was no telling at what time the mine examiners would arrive on their nightly rounds of safety inspection. It was important that all they should find was a big fall of top material—and nothing to show that it was man-made.

Fragments of slate commenced to slip from the roof and fall darkly, slapping into the rubble below. Jojo felt a hard sting across his cheek and he knew that a piece of slate had nipped him. Heavy and sharp, it could cut like a butcher's cleaver. He kept on working—but all at once he dropped the pick.

Something he should have thought of at first . . . With the overhead mass loosened and "alive" for the fall, he scurried under it. In puffing frenzy he tugged until he had Killer Sobczyk's big body on top of Casimir's thin one, covering it everywhere. A coffin lid for Casimir.

Overhead in the "working" roof came a new and deadly note, like pond ice cracking. Jojo heeled backward as slate, top-coal and even some deep rock poured down. Dust swirled . . . the black powder glittered in the lamplight, blotting out everything except the grinding and the clatter.

Jojo pounded his lamp against the heel of his hand to stir up the carbide in the carbide chamber. The flame tongued out, white-hot and hissing. He played the light anxiously into the settling dust. His main concern now was that the fall should be a big one. With this territory almost worked out and soon to be abandoned, the coal company would not pay much money to clean it up. The face boss of the South side would not send Bug-dust Hartley and his cleanup gang in here to shovel up a big fall. A little one, yes. A big one, no.

Gradually the pile of debris took shape inside the pall of dust. It was, Jojo estimated, about a thirty-car fall.

A thirty-car fall was a big one, and satisfaction put a dry brightness in Jojo's eyes. A funeral he had made for Casimir—his grave safe from violation, never to be wet down by woman's not meant tears.

Now Luba could keep thinking the lies he had told her. She could bite her lips and storm and kick with the rage of a woman deserted by her husband and her lover both.

Let the rest of them in town think what they wanted to. The mine examiner's report would read: "Thirty-car fall of slate and top-coal with some rock in the 2d crosscut between Rooms 4 and 5, in the 16th East off the 4th South." This would be the nearest thing to a death certificate that would ever be recorded for two men.

Knowing nothing of the truth, never dreaming that he had fought and killed the Killer, they would bark at him and call him Dog-face the same as always.

Let them. Maybe it had mattered before, only because Jojo knew in his heart that he *was* Dog-face. Now he was—giant killer, yes. Lonesome giant killer. But maybe not always lonesome. There were women not like Luba. A man who was not Dog-face in his heart could maybe one day—like Casimir said—"find good woman for make nice home away from boardinghouse." Why not?

He turned and started on his long walk back to the air shaft. There would be just time to get on top and clean up and go to the saloon for one or two drinks and a cigar before he went to bed.

Bibliography of Books
By Ryerson Johnson

Western Novels:

South to Sonora. New York: Samuel Curl, 1946.
Barb Wire. New York: Arcadia, 1947.

Historical Novel:

Mississippi Flame. Greenwich, Conn.: Red Seal, 1953.

Contemporary Novel:

Nicky (with Winfred Van Atta). New York: Paul S. Eriksson, 1965.

Mystery Novels:

Naked in the Streets. Greenwich, Conn.: Red Seal, 1952.
Lady in Dread. Greenwich, Conn.: Gold Medal, 1955.

Mystery Novels with Davis Dresser, as by Matthew Blood:

The Avenger. Greenwich, Conn.: Gold Medal, 1952.
Death Is a Lovely Dame. Greenwich, Conn.: Gold Medal, 1954.

Mystery Novels as by Brett Halliday:

Dolls are Deadly. New York: Torquil, 1960.
Killer from the Keys. New York: Torquil, 1960.

Pulp Adventure Novels as by Kenneth Robeson:

The Fantastic Island. New York: Bantam, 1966. Originally
published in *Doc Savage Magazine*, 1935.
Land of Always-Night. New York: Bantam, 1966. Originally published in *Doc Savage Magazine*, 1935.
The Motion Menace. New York: Bantam, 1971. Originally
published in *Doc Savage Magazine*, 1938.

Young Adult Adventure Novels:

The Trail of the Deadly Image. New York: Collier, 1963.
The Trail of the Golden Feather. New York: Collier, 1963.
The Trail of the Moaning Ghost. New York: Collier, 1963.
The Trail of the Witchwood Treasure. New York: Collier,
1963.

Nonfiction:

The Art and Skill of Getting Along with People (with Syl-
vanus Duvall). Englewood Cliffs, N.J.: Prentice
Hall, 1961.

Children's Books:

Gozo's Wonderful Kite. New York: Crowell, 1951.
Fives at School (with Elenora Haegele Moore). New York:
Putnam's, 1959.

The Monkey and the Wild Wild Wind. New York: Abelard
    Schuman, 1961.
Let's Walk Up the Wall. New York: Holiday House, 1967.
The Mouse and the Moon. Eau Claire, Wis.: E. M. Hale,
    1968.
Upstairs and Downstairs. New York: Crowell, 1969.
I Like Dinosaurs. Eau Claire, Wis.: E. M. Hale, 1971.
Susi Did It. Lexington, Mass.: Ginn & Co., 1973.
Monsters that Move Earth. Lexington, Mass.: Ginn & Co.,
    1973.
Let's Play Dinosaur. Alameda, Calif.: Front Row Expe-
    rience, 1978.
Icky-Sticky. Alameda, Calif.: Front Row Experience, 1980.
Why is Baby Crying? Chicago: Albert Whitman, 1989.

A Note about the Author

Ryerson Johnson's remarkable literary career enters its eighth decade and sixty-fifth year with the publication of this collection of his best Western stories. Since 1926 he has contributed hundreds of short stories and articles to such magazines as *Collier's, Maclean's, Coronet, Parents' Magazine, Scholastic, Western Story,* and *Argosy*; numerous language arts pieces to educational publishers; teleplays to such TV series as *Death Valley Days*; and comic-book storylines and dialogue for such magazines as *Batman*. He has written fiction and non-fiction books for young people (one of which, *The Monkey and the Wild Wild Wind*, was the recipient of the Jane Addams Award from the Women's International League for Peace and Freedom), a self-help book and several mystery, western, historical, and mainstream novels for adults. He has also served as text editor for publications ranging from pulp magazines to Encyclopedia Britannica's sixteen-volume set of *Young Children's Encyclopedia*.